Good News—I Failed
A Story of Inventing in Minnesota

Good News—I Failed

A Story of Inventing in Minnesota

D. P. Cornelius

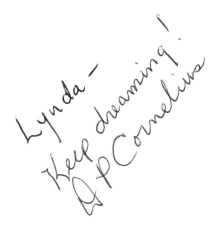

Lynda—
Keep dreaming!
DP Cornelius

Mill City Press, Inc.
212 3rd Avenue North, Suite 290
Minneapolis, MN 55401
612.455.2294
www.millcitypublishing.com

Cover illustrations from Dreamstime.com. Lightbulb (Mitch1921) and
respectively from twelve o'clock: Andre534, 3dbrained, Alexmillos,
Vectorminator, Oxlock, Ekaterinas, Mimirus, Karelindmitriy, Scusi, and
Jankaliciak.

ISBN-13: 978-1-937600-50-1
LCCN: 2011942851

Cover Design and Typeset by Wendy Arakawa

Printed in the United States of America

This book is dedicated to my father, Richard T. ("Dick") Cornelius, and to all inventors and dreamers, wherever they may be.

Special acknowledgment and thanks to my family – my wife Leslie, son Brian, and daughter Cristina for their feedback and support. Additional gratitude must go to local author Mary Logue for her guidance and mentorship, as well as Jill Oldham for her fine editing.

Preface

I don't think it's any secret – inventing can be downright fun. My dad, with over 180 patents, was fortunate to have a lifetime of fun. And sometimes I got to participate. I'll never forget the twinkle in his eyes when discussing a new idea. I can remember, when I must have been about 7 years old, tagging along to the factory on a Saturday morning, watching him sketch some ideas on a yellow legal pad – a necessary tool of the trade back in those days.

This short fictional novel, about a weekend in the lives of a farmer-turned-inventor grandpa and his grandson, is intended to give you a taste for those kinds of experiences. It should also give you some insight into the challenges of not only inventing, but also fulfilling dreams in general. In the story, the grandpa is trying desperately to invent something, while the grandson has his football dreams dashed, soon to be replaced by some promising ideas around an aquarium filter.

As with most stories, this one draws upon some very personal experiences. A power aquarium cleaning device was a product of one of my own dreams. (It was my one and only patent, and like so many patents, was not commercially successful.) Also, the grandpa in the story was inspired by an experience I had as a teenager with an elderly inventor. He had a small shop on Lyndale Ave. in

Minneapolis through which he was selling his unique Christmas tree stands. I figured my dad would be impressed by some super-engineered new gift I had found, and so went to the shop to check out those stands. The old man took great pride in explaining to me the features of his invention, and was thrilled when I decided to purchase one. After I handed him my check, he studied it, and his face lit up. Pointing to a newspaper clipping on his wall, he asked me if I were related to the person in the article. It was a story about my father. I was awestruck at how some inventor would idolize another inventor just as some young ballplayer would idolize a star catcher. You'll see that Grandpa Ralph in this story is one who idolized all of the Minnesota inventors who preceded him.

More than anything, this book is intended to give you an appreciation for the many contributions of Minnesota's great legacy of inventors. Woven into the storyline are examples of how these inventions impact our lives on a daily basis. Whether it be in the realm of agriculture, industry, aeronautics, information technology, medicine, or just plain fun things – there's a diverse array of Minnesota genius on display every day.

In my research, I was struck by the impact of our inventors throughout history – most particularly during World War II. It's amazing how so many Minnesota inventors were able to quickly advance technology in order to meet the challenges of war. I draw attention to these inventors as representatives of Tom Brokaw's *The Greatest Generation*.

Rather than focus on a comprehensive list of all their accomplishments, I've tried to spotlight the more interesting ones, and

I have pulled in the attributes that reveal the human side of these people, such as a big-picture approach to medical treatment by Earl Bakken (pacemaker), a reverence for inspiration by Robert Page (radar), or a passion for solving world hunger by Nelson Borlaug (enhanced wheat). The intent is to spark the reader's interest in following up with more research. As a jumpstart to that process, at the end of the book I've provided an appendix of profiles of Minnesota's key inventors, based on information from the Minnesota Inventors Hall of Fame (to whom I'm greatly indebted), and other sources. Unfortunately, I was unable to secure reproduction rights for all of their photos.

A few notes of clarification are in order: I've identified a universe of 80 Minnesota inventors who are listed in the appendix – I call them *The Minnesota 80*. By no means do I claim to have captured them all, and I was able to pull only about half into the storyline. Their inclusion should not be taken to imply they are the most important inventors. Secondly, for dramatic effect, I changed the date and circumstances around the twilight years of a key inventor (Page) to align with the dates of the fictional story.

In her foreword to Stephen George's book, *Enterprising Minnesotans: 150 Years of Business Pioneers*, Marilyn Nelson Carlson, referring to elements that guided the entrepreneurs, raises a point that would certainly also apply to these inventors (many of whom ultimately became entrepreneurs). She stated, "But there is another element as well: faith. Be it faith in a dream, faith in the future, or faith in God, those who have succeeded here have all had a faith in something larger than themselves or the here and now. That is another Minnesota trait."

No doubt, quite a bit has changed over the years. Much of the manufacturing for the companies started by these inventors has been moved elsewhere. But while the factories may have closed, we can still reminisce about the significant role those inventions have played in both Minnesota and world history. I'm sure that over the years all of Minnesota's fine inventors have carved out wonderful stories, creating lasting memories. Mine go back to a Saturday morning, and a yellow sketch pad. But it's not just the great memories and pride that live on. No doubt, somewhere in Minnesota today, new dreams are being hatched as well.

Chapter One

Checking on Grandpa

Good News – I Failed: A Story of Inventing in Minnesota.

"Begin today. Carry out a random act of seemingly senseless kindness, with no expectation of reward or punishment. Safe in the knowledge that one day, someone somewhere might do the same for you."
– Diana, Princess of Wales

The airplane's wheels finally touched ground with a thud. It was the best of sounds; it was the worst of sounds. So I'm borrowing from *A Tale of Two Cities* – would Mrs. Freeman like that, or would she hate it? Thanks to you, God, for getting me here safely. A pox on you, Dad, for making me come. "Look at it as an adventure," he had said. Yeah, sure – thanks a lot, Dad. You've put me through this horrendous storm-battered flight, after a night of no sleep, and you've messed up all my plans. Just when I had things all set — football practice was done and I was going to the State Fair with my buddies – you have me doing a completely different gig, flying all the way to Sioux Falls just so I can visit my Grandpa Ralph. What does a 14-year-old do with his grandpa for three days?

1

I walked up the ramp to find Grandpa. There he was, standing a bit in the background. I spotted him easily, though, his imposing figure topped by a head of white hair — wavy tufts pushing out the sides beneath an overly tight, dirty-brimmed, *Twins* baseball cap. His face stood in stark contrast, tanned from a summer's worth of sun. I made my way over to him, and we exchanged a hug. Grandpa Ralph was a tall man, well built, and from the hug I could tell there was still a lot of well-toned muscle holding together that 69-year-old frame. I was hoping he would notice the same of me – what with football conditioning and all.

"Great to see you, Josh," he said, giving me a quick once-over. "You look good. A bit pale, maybe, but solid. Have you been working out?" (Hearing that was more than music to my ears – it was *The Star Spangled Banner* before a big ballgame. Yep, I needed something to help get me out of my funk.) He continued, "Have you started practice for the fall football season? What position do you play now?"

"Yeah, in fact we had a long practice yesterday," I replied while readjusting the bag strap that was digging into my shoulder. "I'm a receiver. It's already cut-down time, and I'm worried because I dropped a few balls – that's not like me."

"Well, it must be tough being a receiver when you're what, 5'5?"

"Give me another half inch. I need everything I can get," I replied.

As we walked outside, I was immediately hit by a wall of thick air – much warmer than what I had left in the Twin Cities, but not all that unusual for late August in Sioux Falls. We quickly found Grandpa's pickup truck – a dark green extended-cab Ford F-150. The same one I recall from a year ago when we were all down for his pacemaker surgery. Looked as though it had a few more miles on it – that's for sure. It wasn't long before we were on our way – headed due east about 40 minutes to the farm near Luverne, Minnesota.

On the radio I could hear some guy hyping the new movie, *There's Something about Mary*, claiming it was the best comedy of 1998. That reminded me – that movie had been on the list I had had to abandon – the list of things I wanted to do with my buddies. But my mind soon went back to that horrible flight. I kept thinking about the plane pitching back and forth. The storm must have been a result of the hot muggy air clashing with the cool air from the east. Only wish they hadn't duked it out over my air space. As if he could read my mind, Grandpa piped in, "So how was your flight, Josh?"

"Oh, don't even ask," I moaned, almost before he could finish his sentence. "I think that's why I must look like a ghost. I've never been on such a horrible flight before, and in such a small plane – there were times when I thought we were done for. I sure hope it's better when I fly back."

"I can see why you're glad to be back on the ground," said Grandpa. "You can thank some aeronautical engineers who became Minnesota Hall of Fame Inventors for helping. Just think — if you were the pilot of that plane being knocked around every which way, you'd want to know something about the air pressure and temperature around you and how level the plane is compared to the ground, right? Well, some guys from Rosemount and Honeywell, Mr. Frank Werner and Mr. D. Gilman Taylor, invented those kinds of instruments. Mr. Joseph Killpatrick developed the ring laser gyroscope for navigation. Later on, Ms. Carol Ford made gyroscopes even better. Chances are you made it through because of instrumentation designed or inspired by all of them."

The furthest thing from my mind was the names of a bunch of inventors. Was this what the weekend was going to be – talking about some old people? If they weren't dead yet, they were probably at least doing time in nursing homes. But since it was still early in our getting reacquainted, I decided I would try to be on my best behavior. "Interesting," I responded. "I usually just take that kind of thing for granted. I don't know any of the history behind those inventions." I thought for a second. "Come to think of it, I don't even know what a gyroscope is supposed to do."

"Oh, it measures rotation, giving pilots an indication of how level they are flying in relation to the ground. It's really something how a gyroscope seems to defy gravity. I've got some books I can show you about it," he said. "But don't get hung up on the complicated inventions. Let's not forget that Minnesota inventors have made a big difference with some pretty simple stuff we use every day."

"Like what?" I asked, figuring I would see where Grandpa's line of conversation was headed. I had forgotten how knowledgeable he was about this stuff.

"For example – what did you have for breakfast this morning?"

"Cocoa Puffs and toast," I replied.

"Well, the technology behind puffed cereal, using high pressure and super heated steam, was developed by Dr. Alexander Anderson. Food "shot from guns" was the big hit at the 1904 World's Fair in St. Louis. It was first considered a treat like popcorn. Later on, Mr. Takuzo Tsuchiya from General Mills improved the process and contributed many other inventions so that we can all chow down on ready-to-eat cereals today without much bother.

"Also, did you know that the pop-up toaster was invented by a Minnesotan? In 1929, Mr. Charles Strite received a patent for it, and wouldn't you know a year later Wonder Bread decided to sell sliced bread. It was like a marriage made in heaven – toaster sales skyrocketed. Funny thing how that timeline became a reference point – everyone's heard the expression 'the greatest thing since sliced bread.'"

"Say, Grandpa, I noticed you use the title "Mister" when introducing all those guys. Just wondering – any reason for that?"

"Just me – a respect thing, I guess," he answered, scratching his head. "I admire all these people so much. I use it out of habit when first bringing up their names. I have a hunch you'll be hearing a lot more before the weekend is over – aren't you lucky!" He grinned. "Y'know, I've always had an interest in these inventors' dreams, accomplishments, and the history of it all – especially when they have Minnesota roots."

Just then, as we came around a bend, we saw a car in the distance pulled over to the side. It was in a spot where the shoulder dropped off rather steeply. Grandpa started to slow down. It was a big old blue Buick – I'm sure the largest model Buick ever made – with only the driver inside. Rather a big boat of a car, I would say. In fact it was listing so badly, I feared it could do a *Titanic* on us and roll over at any moment.

"Here, Grandpa –I have a cell phone that my dad loaned me. We can call for help."

"No, Grandson. I think *we'll* do the helping."

As we pulled closer, he said, "For a minute I thought that was Doris Waite from church. But no, I think she's a complete stranger – nobody from around these parts. Looks like she has a flat tire on the right, but we can't change it until we move the car to more level ground. I've got a mini air compressor in the back that can help inflate the tire so we can move the car."

"You shouldn't be doing this kind of work, Grandpa. Dad tells me your heart condition has taken a turn for the worse lately."

"You're right, Josh. I was thinking *you* would be doing the work, but maybe you don't know much about it. Have you ever watched your dad change a tire?"

"Oh, yeah, but without paying too much attention, I must admit."

"Well, this time, by actually doing it, you'll remember," said

Grandpa. Sounded strangely like something my dad would have said.

Grandpa greeted the stranded motorist, and she was more than thrilled to have us help her out. Once we had moved the car forward to more level ground, we pulled the spare tire and jack out of the well of the trunk. Next Grandpa had me look for the right place to attach the jack to the car frame. I was pleased with myself for being able to figure that out. All told, with his expert guidance, the tire changing went well, and not too long thereafter, we were all on our way.

"You, know, Josh, there're some other things I can teach you about tires, too."

I had a feeling this wasn't the only lesson I was going to get from this exercise. "Is there another Minnesota inventor involved?" I volleyed back.

"You bet – how did you guess? Dr. Izaak Kolthoff led a large research group during World War II that developed synthetic rubber that changed the whole tire industry. That's why those tires are still on that car in the first place. Natural rubber tires lasted only about 10,000 miles, as opposed to the 40,000 to 80,000 we get today."

There was a bit of silence as Grandpa continued to motor along, putting some of that mileage on his own tires. Finally he broke in with: "So, Josh, how have you been keeping yourself busy this summer?"

"Well, I had a part-time job at McDonald's, and we went up to a friend's lake cabin in July, but the last week or so it's been all football practice. Making the team has been a dream of mine."

"You went to the lake? Did you do any fishing or water skiing?"

"Yep – we did some water skiing, and that was a lot of fun. The Walkers got a bigger motor for their boat this year. It is so exhilarating to get up on those skis. You're going so fast – seems like you're just skimming across the tops of the waves, ready to go airborne at any moment."

"There's another one for you," interjected Grandpa. "Someone just a few years older than you – an 18-year-old Minnesotan by the name of Mr. Ralph Samuelson – invented water skis back in 1922. He figured that if you could ski on snow, you could do it on water as well, and it's all history after that. Funny thing, though, he never bothered to patent them because he didn't know what he had.

"Yeah – there's all kinds of fun things invented by Minnesotans," he went on. "I've given you some of them as Christmas presents through the years. You were pretty young when you got the *Cootie* game invented by a postman, Mr. W. Herbert Schaper, and some Tonka trucks developed by Mr. Edward Streater. Then there was all the Nerf stuff – remember that Nerf football I gave you? Who knows – maybe that sparked your love of football. It was invented by Mr. Reyn Guyer in 1972. That idea started when his team was horsing around the office with some foam packing materials. I'll bet you also still have the inline skates I sent you. But I bet you didn't know that two brothers, Mr. Scott and Mr. Brennan Olsen, created those in 1980 based on a pair of old-fashioned inline skates they found. And remember when the family used to go fishing up at the lake? We used a few Lindy rigs or two. They were invented by Mr. Ron and Mr. Al Lindner. Back in the day, we all had some good times fishing together, didn't we?"

"Yep, we sure did – and that's quite a collection of fun stuff. I remember them all," I said. I was starting to get pretty interested in these stories. "Just think how totally awesome it would be to have all those inventors locked into a room together. Who knows what they would have come up with! Maybe some really cool video game, ahead of their time."

"Well, they probably would have pushed each other until they came up with something quite unique," replied Grandpa. "Sometimes you just need the right atmosphere for ideas to take hold."

"Yeah, I think I know what you mean," I said. "I'd love to think up something fun, but at home it's a battle to get Dad to even hear me out. I feel like he's always putting down any of my ideas. To him, they're just wild dreams that could never be turned into anything worthwhile, anyway."

My mind drifted to some conversations with Dad that had turned into nothing more than dead ends. It was sure a different atmosphere here with Grandpa. It had become quite obvious that it didn't take much to get him excited about talking about Minnesota inventors. I had always known he was a tinkerer, but I didn't realize until today that he's a walking encyclopedia as well. I guess that's something I hadn't really thought much about before. A lot of fond memories were beginning to roll around in my head, going back to when I was 7 to 10 years old, like the fishing trips. Maybe it wasn't going to be so bad being here after all. One thing was for sure – it wouldn't take much to get Grandpa to tell me what he had on his mind, but even more important, it wouldn't be hard for me to tell him what was on mine.

Just a bit further down the road, we came to the turn to the farm. The corn stood tall on expansive flat land, stretching far from west to east, interrupted only by a row of tall trees shadowing two distant structures at the end of a long driveway. Anchored sturdily at the entry was an awkward mailbox of sorts – no doubt custom built by my grandpa. With its huge, hat-like shroud; jutting, jaw-like receptacle; and angular arms, it was no doubt doing double duty as a scarecrow, maybe even more successfully than as a mailbox.

Chapter Two

Getting Settled

*"Dreams are renewable. No matter what our age
or condition, there are still untapped possibilities within
us and new beauty waiting to be born."*
— Dale Turner, Minnesota-born trumpeter

As we approached the farmhouse, I couldn't help but wonder why they always put the buildings so far from the highway, so I asked Grandpa.

"Well, that's a good question, Grandson. My father built this house, so I'm not really sure. Maybe a privacy thing, maybe the lay of the land. Even though I was born and raised in the house, I never thought to even ask him. So you're already a step ahead of me."

We pulled up to the building located on the east side of the house. It was a large structure, a combination garage and workshop. I imagined Grandpa spent a lot of time inside there. We were immediately greeted by a black lab, Grandpa's dog, Sally, who wagged her tail nonstop. The only sound she made, though, was some welcoming whimpers – no doubt she recognized Grandpa's truck.

Opposite the workshop, to the west, was a straight row of trees – tall soldiers dutifully protecting the farm from any nasty weather, especially from any frontal attack by the strong northwesterly winds. On this particular day in August, however, they were no match against the high sun's rays that beat steadily down upon us. Immediately to the east of the trees was the farmhouse, an old two-story structure, white clapboard, with chocolate-brown shingles. The shutters were a matching brown. With my stomach already starting to growl from hunger, it was easy to imagine Kit Kat bars plastered to the wall. But the stomach must not have been too connected to the brain (which would have told it they'd be long since melted, among other things). A lingering disconnect, I'm sure, from the stormy skies far above Sioux Falls.

I noticed that next to the workshop was a small loader. It was an older Bobcat, looking like it had seen better days, but I was sure it was in excellent mechanical condition.

"Oh, I got that used – real cheap," said Grandpa, clearly proud of the hard bargain he had driven. "Comes in very handy for plowing the snow out of that long driveway, among other things. Did you know some Minnesotans came up with that?"

"I should have known." I smiled as I bent down to give Sally a few pats on the head.

"Yeah, two brothers from the farm country invented the first four-wheel-drive skid-steer loader – Mr. Cyril Keller and Mr. Louis Keller. You see Bobcats used all over the place these days. They turn on a dime. *Fortune* magazine once put the Bobcat on its top

100 list of 'America's Best.'"

"So, can we take a look in the workshop?" I asked, nodding my head over in that direction.

"Oh, no – not yet, Josh. I've been working on my own invention. It's coming along real good, and I want to surprise you with a demonstration while you're here."

"Your own invention? Awesome!" But suddenly I remembered he had told me that before – how could I have forgotten? "Oh, that's right," I continued. "You mentioned it last time we were down. What is it? Give me at least a clue, will ya?"

"No – you'll see it in due time. Just be patient.

"So, Josh – can you help me bring in the groceries and supplies behind the seats? There's some fresh deli meats and bread – let's whip up a sandwich or two."

Walking into the house, it seemed like not much had changed since about a year ago when we were all last down. Grandpa wasn't the neatest of people, and I could see some tufts of Sally's hair that had found comfortable spots near the lower edges of the green sofa and tucked into the cushions of the plaid easy chair. I had the feeling that the house had not been thoroughly cleaned since Grandma died two years ago. To add to the not-so-welcoming feeling, it was really hot inside.

"Josh, since you're 'company,' as they say, let's splurge and turn on the air conditioner. I think all the windows are closed, but we'd better double check. The thermostat is over there on the hall-way wall – the round Honeywell one. Can you go put it on while I put these groceries away?"

I was all in favor of that, and went to check the windows and locate the thermostat.

"That's another Minnesota invention right there," Grandpa yelled out. "Mr. Carl Kronmiller, 'Mr. Thermostat' himself, im-proved an earlier concept by Mr. Albert Butz and came up with the familiar round one. He also pioneered the idea of a pilot flame and a button as a safety feature while opening up the main burner. It's been said that at some point just about every home in America has had one of those thermostats."

No sooner had we sat down at the table for lunch when the phone rang. Just like at home, I thought to myself.

"Oh, hello, Bert – how are you doing? Yes, I'm fine," said Grandpa. "Just sitting down to eat, but that's all right. What's up? Well, I can help you, but I have my grandson here this weekend, so it won't be until next week. What's that? The wheel bearing on your tractor? Yeah, I've swapped out a few of those in my day – no problem. I'll be over Monday morning to help you out. Does that work for you? Well, okay, see you then."

"That's Bert Sanders down the road a bit. Seems like I'm al-ways helping him out with something."

We started in on our sandwiches. Grandpa soon piped up: "It's great to spend some quality time with you, but to be honest, I was hoping it would be more than just you and me here together. I wish it could have been your folks, too – my Karen and your dad, even though the divorce has messed everything up. I'd have settled for your dad and stepmom, too. You know, it seems like I never get to see anyone much anymore. Everyone's always so busy." He chewed for a bit, swallowed, and then continued. "So they sent you down to check up on me, huh?"

"Well, yeah, I guess. That's true – they are awfully busy these days," I stammered, as he caught me off guard.

But it was all still fresh in Grandpa's mind. "Well, when I called your dad last week, he didn't seem to have a whole lot of time for me," he said. "And now that I think back, maybe I made it sound like my situation is worse than it really is."

"Oh, so it was you who called Dad? I thought it was the other way around, with Dad checking up on you. Well, I'm glad I could make it down," I said, trying to apply some salve to what seemed like a festering sore spot. I figured maybe now was a good time to get it all out. "Y'know, it was really Mom's idea," I went on. "She called Dad from her new place in Ohio and asked him if it wouldn't be a good idea to check on you in person, what with your heart problems flaring up. He didn't have time, so he sent me down. You must have been talking to Mom as well, right?"

"Yeah, I've talked to both of them. You know, it's just not the same, especially now, with my Rose gone." Grandpa sighed heavily and shook his head. "I'm still trying to stay connected. And now that your mom's moved so far away with her new husband,

I'm trying to get things started back up with your dad, but it hasn't gone real well."

"Everyone's just so busy," I said, trying again to smooth things over. I thought it was best to change the subject. As I cast about for a new topic, I got a little help from a newscaster I heard on the radio in the background. "With today being the 35th anniversary of Dr. Martin Luther King's 'I Have a Dream' speech, President Clinton is expected to..."

"So, Grandpa, cool – this is 'I Have a Dream Day.' Does that lift your spirits and make you think of your dreams?"

"I suppose," he responded. "Dreams come in all shapes, sizes, and flavors. Mine have to do with inventing. They don't really have anything to do with the kind of things Martin Luther King was trying to do. He was in a whole different league."

"Yeah, so Grandpa, maybe now would be a good time to make plans. What sort of things should we do this weekend?"

"Well, you don't fly out until late on Sunday, right?"

"Yeah, I think my flight is about 8:00 p.m. – I'll have to check my ticket to be sure. That means we'd better head out no later than 5:30, right?"

"That's right. I was thinking you'd come to church with me Sunday and then stay afterward for our annual summer potluck. I'd like to reintroduce you to some of my friends. It's a wonderful time to visit, and of course the food is always terrific. You'll be so full, you won't even be thinking of any dinner later on."

"Will there be any kids my age there?" I was already starting to dread a whole afternoon with a bunch of folks who were so old that when *Super Mario* first came out, they probably thought it was the extra large version you ordered from Pizza Hut.

"Well, I suspect so," replied Grandpa, "but you'll have to reach out to them. As for tomorrow," he went on, "I thought maybe you could help shuck the corn. I've agreed to bring a lot of ears. You could do that while you're watching the football game. Are the Gophers playing?"

"No, not until next week, but I'm sure there's some other game on. Yeah, okay, I'll help with that. Maybe Sunday there will be enough guys around to actually pull together a touch football game."

My lack of sleep was catching up with me. I felt bad about it, but I figured I should be up front. "Grandpa, would you mind if I crashed for a while? I was up really late last night. I'll be much fresher for some good talks tonight," I said.

"Sure – I set you up in your mom's old room upstairs. I don't think she'll be using it anytime soon," he said with a hint of regret. "I'm going to go pick the corn for the potluck in the meantime and then go work on my project. I'll come and get you in an hour or so."

"Oh, I should really help you pick," I said. "I didn't realize you were going to do some work."

"Not a problem – I think I've done it a few times in my life. You go upstairs and get some rest. On second thought, let me go up with you to check it out."

As we entered my mom's old room, I couldn't help but think about what it must have been like for her growing up there. The room was bright as the sun's rays made their way through the coarse, patterned curtains and reflected softly off the yellow walls. A painting on the wall depicting a girl at a flower shop contrasted sharply with its dark blue background. I wondered how long it had been since my mom had been in this very room, perhaps looking at that painting or resurrecting some childhood memories. I threw off my shoes and plopped down onto the large bed, my hands clasped behind my head. Grandpa headed over to the dresser. It was an old-fashioned style but had been painted a modern cream color, no doubt to please a young girl. A picture stood prominently on top, and Grandpa was gazing at it fondly. I peered over that way but couldn't tell who was in it. "Hey, Grandpa, what's that picture all about?" I asked. Wiping off a layer of dust, he studied it for a moment, recollecting, I was sure, a very meaningful occasion. "Oh, this is your folks and me in a fishing boat, back when we did a family trip up to a resort up in Alex. Let's see – that would have been about six years ago. Remember how we did that sort of thing back in those days?"

Memories of being out in the boat must have begun to take over his mind. He started to describe it. "There's nothing like the serenity of the lake in the evening after the winds calm down – the boat rounding a point to enter a quiet bay; the motor sputtering to an idle as the boat slows down, thousands of bubbles rushing to the surface; the trailing wake catching up with the craft as it hunkers lower into the water…"

As Grandpa went on, I closed my eyes and could just about feel the gentle slap, slap, slap of the waves lapping against the hull. I remembered the faint, fleeting smell of the boat's exhaust, heard the plaintive wail of a distant loon. I could picture the sound as the motor shut off: sweet, still silence.

"Those were precious times. Perfect," said Grandpa. He looked about a million miles away.

"Yeah, cool, that is quite a memory," I said. "You get your serenity from going fishing on a quiet lake. It's funny – fish are a part of my serenity times, too. But that would be next to my aquarium. There's nothing like watching them swim peacefully around the rocks in the tanks back home. I can sit there for twenty minutes sometimes. It's a nice break from the video games or football, y'know."

I reflected back to sitting in a chair by the aquarium, gazing at my fish. My favorites are those red wag platies with the black tails. The way their tails wag back and forth – you would think they were some puppy dog that hasn't seen you in ages. Sure, they're just swimming, but as their eyes peer up to the surface for some morsel of food, it seems that they're actually happy to be where they're at. Maybe that's because I've just cleaned the tank, and they really are happy. Could that be? Do fish have feelings? I don't mind taking some credit, anyway, I thought.

My reverie about serenity soon joined the quiet comfort that had enveloped me in my mom's big bed. As my eyes started to close, I noticed Grandpa slipping out of the room. Yes, there was something awfully cozy about that welcoming old bed, as I slept well. Suddenly I was awakened by the buzz of the cell phone in my front pocket. What time is it? I thought. I must have been out for quite a while.

"Hello?" It was my buddy Brad. "Hey, man, what's up?"

Brad cleared his throat on the other end of the line and said, "So, I have some news. I just wanted to let you know."

"Know what?" This didn't sound good. Brad sounded too serious, for one thing. I heard the words through the phone as if in a daze. "What do you mean I didn't make the team? You're messing with me, right?" But I could tell from his voice that he wasn't. Damn. I really hadn't made it.

I found myself racking my brain with 'how could that be' questions while deep down realizing I was not shocked – only extremely disappointed. Those dropped passes. I just had not been on top of my game. "What about Mike and Andy?" I asked.

"Yeah, they made it, man." I could hear the sympathy in Brad's voice. I just couldn't bear to talk about it anymore. "I gotta go," I said, and hung up. Andy? I thought to myself. He's just a big old lineman and has it so easy – just gets in people's way, that's all. He made the team, and I didn't? It's just not fair!

I ran down the stairs and out the back door to let off some steam, pacing back and forth, oblivious to what was going on. I headed toward the front of the house in search of Sally, and found her resting with her head on the front stoop. I sat down beside her, patting her head and stroking her black fur. "It's just not fair," I told her, figuring she most certainly would understand. She looked up at me with sympathetic dark eyes. "I didn't make the team," I said. "All my buddies did, but not me. My dream just got flushed down the toilet." I had a hollow feeling in the pit of my stomach, and it wasn't because I was hungry. I scratched behind Sally's ears. She was wagging her tail, but ever so slowly. "That tail better not mean you're happy, does it?" I asked. She put one paw over the other. "Hey, there you go – are you praying for me? Maybe that's what I need.

"You dogs have really got it easy. Do you have any idea what it feels like? Yeah, maybe when Grandpa didn't give you that steak bone? I can see how that would leave you with a hollow in your stomach too," I said, reaching for a little levity that might snap me out of my funk. I continued to grapple to try to find some peace, gazing out at the cornfields as they stretched before me, but they were a blur. I don't think anyone would say dogs aren't your best companions when you're really down. They listen and never say it was your fault. I looked back at Sally for reassurance. Her eyes were now closed, and her tail was still. I guess it must be time to move on. The world beyond me came back into focus. My attention reverted back to my grandpa's world.

By this time, I thought, he was no doubt working on his invention. I decided I would head over to the workshop to see if I could at least hear what was going on. I noticed the door was closed. I found I was bucking a strong warm breeze as I made my way toward it. It's probably not a good idea to enter, I thought – even the breeze is trying to tell me that.

Chapter Three

Dreams

"Failure is simply the opportunity to begin again,
this time more intelligently."
—Henry Ford, inventor of automobile mass production

I noticed a double-hung window on the side of the workshop. It was open several inches, so I went over to find out what I could see or hear.

The window apparently had not been moved in quite some time, as the sun's rays revealed the silky threads of a substantial spider web. Despite the brisk breeze, the web held strong, all the way from the upper left corner down to the open right corner. As I watched, the spider appeared at the top, as if to say "stay away from my territory." There was not much to see, but there was a strange odor coming from the open window. It was like the smell of spilled oil fermenting with hay. I soon concluded, however, that unlike a fine wine, it wasn't getting any better with age. That strange odor had probably hung around for quite some time, but perhaps that's not that unusual for the farm.

As I listened intently at the window, all I could hear was the ringing sound of a hammer on metal – nary a grunt nor groan from Grandpa. This is silly, I thought. Why not just go and open the door and surprise Grandpa – he wouldn't be too upset, would he? I could use the excuse of having to reveal my disappointing news about not making the football team. After a few seconds of reflection, though, I decided against it. I would let him play out his hand. Besides, I wasn't ready to tell him my news.

Suddenly, it didn't matter, as I heard the door bang open, and my grandpa come running out. I ran around the corner to see what was going on. He was very agitated, yelling and cursing unlike anything I had ever heard from him. "Oh, Josh – you're out here," he said a bit sheepishly, trying to settle himself down. His face was red and he was sweating profusely.

"What's wrong, Grandpa? What's going on? What happened?" I was worried.

"It's totally not working, Josh. What I had expected is just not working. I feel like a failure." As he uttered those words, his right hand reached over to his heart.

"Oh, my God, Grandpa! What's with the hand on your chest? Are you having chest pains?"

"Yeah, Josh. My angina is acting up. I'd better take one of my pills. They're on my dresser up in my bedroom."

"Let's get into the house so you can sit down and rest. I'll get your pills." I put my arm around him for support and hurried him into the house. Plop – he collapsed into his favorite easy chair. In a frenzied state of urgency, I ran for the pills, slipping on the throw rugs all along the way. Rummaging under a bunch of clutter on grandpa's dresser, I finally found the pill container. I rushed back and retrieved a cup of water and a wet cloth from the kitchen. I handed the cup and pill to Grandpa. He swallowed the pill, and I wiped his sweaty brow. The furrows were indeed deep, and many in number. It took a couple of wipes to bring some composure back to his flushed face.

"Do we need to get you to a doctor?"

"I'm doing a bit better – I think the pill is already helping. Let me just rest for a little while." With that, he closed his eyes.

I did not take mine off of him for what seemed like a full ten minutes. I quietly watched his chest move gently in and out with a regularity that gave me great relief.

Then he opened his eyes, leaned forward a bit, and spoke with a quiet, measured voice. "I think I'm going to be okay, and I certainly trust my pacemaker is still doing its job. Mr. Earl Bakken didn't invent no junk, you know. Can you check my pulse to make sure it is steady?"

His pulse felt steady – thank God. "Seems okay, but then I'm no nurse or doctor," I said.

"Good. At least the pill and pacemaker are doing their job for the medical pain in my heart. I can't say that for the other pain. After all this time I've spent on this invention, I can't believe it's still not working." I could see his frustration returning as his pain ebbed.

"Come on, now. You, more than anybody, know the ups and downs of inventing," I tried to sound encouraging.

"Yeah, I know. But this time I thought I was getting close – only to have it fail on the final test. I really thought this weekend it was all going to come together."

"Grandpa, maybe you're putting too much pressure on yourself because I'm here. You should sleep on it, and I'm sure you'll feel better about it in the morning."

"No, it's too early for me to call it a day. Besides, strangely enough, I'm feeling pretty hungry. Do you suppose you could work on some dinner?"

"You bet. What do you have in mind?"

"Well, there's a small side of ham in the refrigerator," he replied. "Throw that into the oven to heat up for awhile, and you've got the start of a good meal. You can also take some of those potatoes out of the freezer. Throw them in the oven for awhile too. Add some green beans, and we're in business. Can you handle that?"

I started to pull things together. My goal was simple – get something on the table. While I worked in the kitchen, Grandpa continued to rest in his chair. Finally, I had dinner ready to throw on the plates. I called Grandpa into the kitchen and we sat down at the table.

"So, Grandpa – how are you doing?" I asked. "Are you sure

you're going to be okay?"

"I'll be fine. I just needed to settle down a bit after the big disappointment. It's hard trying to be an inventor when you're thin on patience like I am. The thing is, I know better. And then I just get mad at myself. Believe it or not, one of my favorite quotes is from Earl Bakken. He said, 'Failure is closer to success than inaction.' I love that quote. I absolutely love it. Now I've just got to live it. I mean, that's the story of an inventor's life. You keep trying until your head is too sore from banging it against the wall. But you learn from each failure, and hopefully your next try is better than the one before."

"But sometimes," I said, "you just don't get there, and that's got to be awfully frustrating, right?"

"That's right, and nobody knows what the timeline is, either. You continually keep asking yourself if the next time will be it."

"Maybe another set of eyes can get you over the hump," I offered. My offer was sincere, but I knew I had an ulterior motive – by this time, I was dying to see what he was working on.

"Well, it's funny how sometimes failures become opportunities for others," Grandpa continued. "Do you know how Post-it notes were invented? Mr. Art Fry of 3M actually ended up using another inventor's failure – an adhesive that didn't stick very well. It all began with him trying to think of a better way to mark the pages in his hymnal without actually marking them. Once he had developed sticky notes that worked, it was a battle to get 3M management to accept the idea. He got them to at least try the notes

for awhile, and they ended up getting addicted. Post-its were introduced to the marketplace in 1980."

"How do you know all these dates off the top of your head,
Grandpa? Where do you get all this information from, anyway?
Books and the Internet?"

"Yes, one of my key resources has been a listing of inductees
into the Minnesota Inventors Hall of Fame – that's right out on the
Internet and provides profiles of each Hall of Famer. The stories
of inventors are just something I have a keen interest in because
I admire what it takes to actually invent something. I also make
trips probably once a month into Sioux Falls and spend the entire
afternoon at the library.

"That's where I've learned," he continued, "about other inventions that came about by accident. Ms. Patsy Sherman was the
research chemist at 3M who came up with the soil repellent that's
now known as Scotchgard fabric protector. I'm sure that's bailed
you out a few times when you've spilled pop on the couch or in the
car. That all started in the lab when someone accidentally spilled
a chemical on an assistant's white tennis shoe. When the chemists
noticed that shoe stayed clean and free of stains, they knew they
were on to something."

I was getting intrigued. "So what are some of the others things
that prompt inventions?"

"Well, nature often gives inventors their ideas," replied Grandpa. "Have you ever noticed how a leaf leaves its imprint on the
snow on a sunny day? Well, Mr. Carl Miller of 3M got an inspira-

tion from it. He realized that the leaf absorbed the radiant heat while the snow reflected the sun's rays, and he had the idea to apply that same idea to paper rolling on a hot drum. From that, Mr. Miller invented the first commercial copy machine, called a Thermo-Fax."

"Sometimes I see seeds falling that remind me of helicopters as they glide to the ground," I thought aloud. "I think those are maple leaf seeds, aren't they? I suppose somebody was inspired by them to invent helicopters."

"Yep, I think you're right – that's a good case in point. As long as we're talking nature, here's another great example. A Swiss engineer by the name of Mr. George de Mestral returned from a walk in a field with so many burrs stuck to his clothing that he decided to take a good hard look at them. He noticed they had hundreds of tiny hooks that caused them to cling. He copied the hooks and matched them with a fabric with tiny loops. You can guess his invention: Velcro."

Cool, I thought, trying to picture what Velcro looks like up close. I could see the similarity.

"A Minnesotan, Dr. Otto Schmitt, came up with one of his great ideas from watching frogs. How do you suppose a frog knows it's going to land on a particular lily pad? Dr. Schmitt figured out that the frog keeps observing its position and sending feedback to its muscles until it has the perfect trajectory. He used that idea to help design self-adjusting electronic feedback circuits that are used in many electronic devices today."

"Man, we studied frogs in science class last year. But I never thought of how they figure out how far to jump. So where is Schmitt's invention used?" I asked.

"Well, his Schmitt trigger, which converts analog signals to digital, can be found in just about every computer today.

"But the example I like the best from nature is the bat," said Grandpa.

"Ugh, bats," I shuddered. "I don't think anyone likes those bad boys. The only kind I like are the ones hanging around a baseball diamond – made of wood or aluminum. That reminds me of a time when I was pretty young, up in the attic with my dad while he was trying to catch a bat. He had a tennis racket in his hand, swinging it wildly, trying to nail this bat that was flying around frantically. I was pretty scared. I didn't know which would hit my head first – the bat or the tennis racket. But, believe me, I was sure hoping it wouldn't be the bat."

"Oh, bats are one of the most misunderstood creatures," Grandpa said earnestly. "They keep the bug population under control. They have some real biological gifts, too. Take the way they find their prey. They constantly send out high-pitched sounds. Those sound waves, which humans can't hear, act like radar, bouncing back to give the exact location depending on which ear hears it louder. It's similar to radar, but with sound instead of radio waves. The process is called echolocation. That's one capable little critter."

The phone rang, and Grandpa reached over to get it.

"Oh, hi, Maureen." ("Speaking of ol' bats," he whispered to me, smiling as he covered the receiver with one hand.) "No, I won't forget, Maureen. I'll bring four folding tables with chairs along with the corn. Frank Albright is also bringing a number of tables. I hope you'll be bringing your scrumptious fried chicken? Fabulous – we'll see you Sunday." He set the phone back in its cradle.

"Josh – wait until you sink your teeth into a piece of Maureen's fried chicken. I'll swear she's found more secret ingredients than the Colonel ever dreamed of. Why, it's almost as good – but note I say *almost* as good – as your grandma's fried chicken. My, how I miss that!" Grandpa breathed in deeply, as if he could almost smell the aroma of Grandma's chicken filling the house.

"I'm all for that – I can't wait." Just a minute, I thought to myself. What was I saying? I hadn't been looking forward to spending an afternoon with all of Grandpa's old friends. I guess I can chalk it up to the promise of good food to get me to change my heart – maybe that will do the trick.

Chapter Four

A Full Day

"They say dreams are the windows of the soul – take a peek and you can see the inner workings, the nuts and bolts."
—*Henry Bromel, television writer*

"Duck," the man in the swim trunks yelled as he came rushing out from behind the corn stalks. Good thing I did, because a big water ski came whizzing through the air just above my head. "Hey! What are you doing?" I yelled. "Just trying to nail that bat that's flying around," the man said. Before I could respond, another guy tapped me on the shoulder. I spun around to see him all dressed up in a blue suit and red tie – with a spinning gyroscope in the palm of his hand. Meanwhile, another guy's got a football in one hand and he's motioning me to go out for a long pass. I go running out into the open field and, stretching my full body out parallel to the ground, I make an absolutely fantastic catch – wish the coaches had seen that one! Shoot. I look down and see that's it's just a Nerf football. At the edge of the cornfield, I see someone else crawling around the ground – looking for something. All of a sudden he holds up a huge bug – it looks like a Cootie, but it's really alive, and its legs are wriggling wildly.

It took something pretty fantastic to wake me up from that dream, and if there's one thing that will do it, it's the aroma of bacon frying in a pan. That delectable smoky wood scent came wafting up into my bedroom, prompting me to get up quickly and head downstairs. Wow, what a dream, I mumbled to myself as I made my way down the stairs.

As I approached the kitchen, I could hear the crackling and popping of those thick slices as they shimmied in the hot pan. Hungry as I was, I hoped they were trying hard not to shrink too much.

"Good morning, Grandpa. That bacon smells awesome. What kind do you buy?"

"Oh, once in a while I ask my cousin from up in Pierz to send me some from Thielen's Meats. They do their own curing, and it's my favorite! We'll fix you up a good farm-style breakfast, with eggs, toast, and all – even though the doc says I need to take it easy on the cholesterol."

"Sounds great," I replied. "We've got this day off to a good start – let's hope it will be better than yesterday afternoon. I had a weird dream last night, though. All those inventors' names were rolling around in my head, and I was dreaming of you picking the corn for the potluck when all of a sudden, some guys appeared among the stalks and started talking to you. It reminded me of that movie, *Field of Dreams,* when those ballplayers come walking out of the cornfields onto the ball field, but these guys were different – they were inventors." I shook my head to clear it. "Did you ever see that movie?"

"Yeah, that was a terrific movie," Grandpa responded. "So did you play ball with them?"

"Well, not exactly." I went on to describe the dream in a bit more detail.

"That's one crazy dream," replied Grandpa. "So what was I doing in the dream all that time?"

"Oh, you were quietly picking ears of corn, but then in the end they all came over to show you a better way to do it! That's what inventors usually do, right?"

"Yep, I guess you're probably right," he chuckled as he set a plate of bacon and eggs on the kitchen table in front of me.

"I remember when my dad rented that movie," I said. "We had a great time watching what's turned out to be one of the greatest baseball stories ever. I still like football better, though. That's really my favorite sport."

"So, football it is, huh?" asked Grandpa. "What player is your role model?"

"Rod Smith of the Denver Broncos. Definitely."

"No one from the Vikes? What's wrong with you, boy? They should have a super team this year," Grandpa chided. "What is it about Smith that you like?"

"Oh, I still root for the Vikings, for sure, and you're right, this may be their year. It's just that Rod came from nowhere and stands for a lot of things I admire. He's not that tall for a receiver. He went to a Division II college. Did you know he wasn't even drafted by the pros? He was able to catch on his first year with the Patriots, but then he was released. He just kept working hard until he landed with a great team, the Broncos. Since then he's had a great career."

"Kind of like the underdog who's made it big," said Grandpa. "Something about human nature – I think most people like to root for those who really work at something and then achieve it. People with that kind of dedication are bound to succeed."

I figured it was time to break the news. "Well, okay," I began haltingly. "I had a bad day yesterday, too, Grandpa. With everything going on, I didn't tell you that I got a call from one of my buddies. I didn't make the football team."

There was a lingering silence. "So your dream got dashed too," said Grandpa. "Not a good day for dreams, I would say." I saw the understanding look on his face, and I could tell he really knew how upset I was.

"No, I guess we both hit a wall on 'I Have a Dream Day,'" I said. "It just doesn't seem fair."

"Well, that's the nature of dreams and inventions," he replied. "Our time will come – just on a different day. I know it's not easy," he went on, "but it doesn't mean you can't benefit from what's happened in the past. It's all a learning process. Where can you go from here? Think about Rod Smith. What was it you said you admire about him? His hard work and reliability, and the way he always uses his abilities to the fullest, right? If you can pattern yourself after him, and combine those traits with your God-given talent, I think you just may find some success.

"I'll tell you what," he went on. "Maybe to get our minds off of our dashed dreams, we should dig into the corn shucking project. Did you see those bushel baskets I left outside by the door? Sorry to say there are lots of ears of corn there – enough to feed the whole church. After you get cleaned up for the day, let's haul them inside and we'll get started. That way we can watch football when it comes on and kill two birds with one stone."

"Sounds good," I said, as I gathered up the dishes. "Say, that was a mighty tasty breakfast – thanks."

"Well, not as good as what your grandma would have made," he replied. "She was quite the cook. Cooks are inventors, too, you know. If they can pull together a bunch of ingredients ever so carefully, we all get to benefit with something absolutely heavenly. I can smell her French toast now, with that little bit of nutmeg in it. When you think about it, she was a better inventor than I've been. I really do miss her."

"Yeah, I know how you feel. I miss her too," I replied. Grandpa sighed as he headed upstairs. I finished cleaning up in the kitchen. While wiping down the counter I noticed a bulletin board on the wall with various things pinned to it. Next to some receipts, an old newspaper clipping stood out as it was markedly yellow in color and rough on the edges. The title read, "Cottonwood Man Wins Grand Prize at Inventor's Show." I did a quick read and made a mental note to ask Grandpa more about it later.

*   *   *   *   *

After getting cleaned up for the day, we got started on the project. As I slowly peeled the husk from one of the ears of corn, Grandpa gave me one of those looks.

"City boy – that's no way to shuck corn. You can't just go one piece of husk at a time – it will take you forever. Let me show you how it will go much faster."

"What, are you going to be like those inventors in my dream, and show me a better way?" I kidded him.

"Yep," he said without hesitation, and proceeded to demonstrate. He picked up an ear, and with each hand pulled as much of the husk and silk together in one motion as he could. Within seconds it was clean – completely naked, with its plump, creamy yellow kernels totally exposed to the whole wide world. Man, that was slick. I tried a few more, and I could see that I needed to develop a better technique or this would be an awfully long project. Oh, well, there was plenty of opportunity to practice. There were hundreds of ears to shuck – at least that's what it looked like to me.

After a while, as we watched the football game on Grandpa's old-style box TV, the shucking got to be pretty tedious, and despite his skill and speed, we still had several dozen to do. I suddenly had a revelation. "Hey, I can guess what invention you've been working on," I said. "I'll bet it's a handy corn shucker. I can see it now, advertised on TV. 'But wait, there's more – if you order in the next five minutes, we'll send you two Super Shuckers for the price of one, plus only a small shipping and handling charge. But, hurry, you must act now.'"

"Hey, maybe you've got a good idea there," Grandpa chuckled. "But no, that's not it."

"Ah, just tell me. Please?"

"Well, considering what happened yesterday, since it's not going to come together this weekend, I might as well tell you. It's a type of quick-connect hydraulic power hitch for tractors. It should save farmers some time and effort."

"Oh, wow," I tried to sound supportive, but maybe I was expecting some miracle invention, and it came across in my voice. I tried to quickly recover. "Sounds like the farming inventions are the ones that you really dig, right?"

"You got it. I like the guys who have come from a farming background, often starting from nothing, and have created major products that contribute to agriculture. I really admire what they have done. There are a few inventors in particular that are near and dear to my heart."

"So tell me about them."

"Well, I like the farmers who turned into inventors, like Mr.

Floyd Buschbom. He contributed bale loaders and silo unloaders, all to make his life as a farmer, as well as mine, much easier."

"So what is it about him that you like so much?" I was giving Grandpa a taste of his own medicine, but he was on a roll and didn't seem to notice.

"Well, for one, he's a local boy from southern Minnesota, and I'm impressed by how persistent he's been. He's accumulated over 100 U.S. and Canadian patents. Another inventor from southwest Minnesota, who goes back a few years, is Mr. Adolph Ronning. He invented the Ensilage harvester. Patented in 1915, it would cut corn, grind it into silage, then store it in a pulled wagon – it became a standard. There are other more recent local boys, too, who have participated in the Inventors Congress right up in Redwood Falls. Mr. Harold Fratzke is always one to beat as he's been at it for many years and has won before. There's an article about him on the bulletin board in the kitchen."

"Oh, yeah – I just noticed that article. Cool. So what is the Inventors Congress?"

"It's a nonprofit organization set up way back in 1958 – they say it's the largest continuously run show of its type. Inventors come to share their inventions, and the show sponsors give out awards. That's where I'm going to bring my invention next June.

"Another thing," he went on, "that I really like about some of the agricultural guys is they are so down to earth with their focus on people, rather than on just making a profit. Take, for example, Mr. Ebenhard Gandrud, known as Gandy. He accumulated 80 patents related to the accurate application of chemicals and fertilizers. Gandrud's company profile spells out the importance of service to mankind through increased food production."

"It's nice to see that the ultimate goal is to create more food at a lower cost," I said. "Hunger is a worldwide problem that we'll be dealing with for years to come. We've talked about it a lot in social studies. Some of us have even volunteered to pack meals for *Feed My Starving Children*."

My mind traveled back to the experience of packing the meals. We were all standing around a table scooping dry rice, soy protein, dehydrated vegetables, chicken flavoring, and vitamins and minerals into a funnel that filled a plastic bag. I got to do the weighing and sealing of the bags, and we all encouraged each other to keep it moving as fast as possible. I'm sure some machine could actually do it faster, but there's nothing like the experience of actually packing the meals for some starving kids across the other side of the world.

"It's really kids feeding kids," I added. "And many of these bags of food are distributed at schools. What better way to encourage the kids to get to school?"

"Right on," Grandpa replied, then continued: "Well, thanks to new technologies and the use of modern production practices, our farmers have done their part by just about doubling their productivity in the last five decades."

"Another guy I've heard a lot about through school is Norman Borlaug," I said. "Now, that guy really made some big-time contributions."

"So, you know all about Dr. Borlaug? Terrific," replied Grandpa. "Did you know he is the only agricultural scientist to win a Nobel Prize? It was way back in 1970, I believe, so maybe you hadn't heard about that."

"Yeah, I had. But I forget the details behind what he did to earn it."

"His claim to fame," responded Grandpa, "was developing a new type of 'semi-dwarf' wheat strain that was stubbier but could hold much larger seed heads. It worked really well with fertilizer and was better suited for underdeveloped countries. On top of that, it was super resistant to diseases.

"Through his hard work in countries like Mexico, India, and Pakistan, farmers there were able to triple and quadruple their production, saving millions and millions of people from starvation. What's more, most of those countries eventually became self-sufficient and didn't have to keep importing wheat.

"Another thing I like about him," continued Grandpa, "is that he was my type of guy – such a 'hands-on' fellow, spending years in the fields in those countries training young scientists. No doubt about it – you've got to put him high on the list of those making a difference to mankind. Also, for you sports-minded guys, he helped set up a Little League while he was in Mexico and coached a team that made it to the championship round."

I imagined being a player on that team. I'm sure the fields were nowhere near as nice as what we have. No green grass, no regular bases, no foul lines, no fences. I pictured myself being picked up by Mr. Borlaug on the way to baseball practice, a well-worn mitt planted on my left hand. The back of his station wagon would no doubt be filled with plants. Little would I know that those were probably the beginnings of plants that would someday feed the world. Little would I know that I was actually riding with a future Nobel Prize winner.

Grandpa continued with the conversation. "Getting back to the mechanical side, which is more my area, another inventor who had a worldwide impact was Mr. Frank Donaldson. He started out in agriculture, but his products grew to have a lot more uses. He invented the first commercial air cleaners and filters for things like tractors and combine engines. That expanded so that the company is now the world's largest manufacturer of heavy duty air cleaners for not only tractors, but also trucks – not to mention construction and military purposes. Donaldson Company now employs over 10,000 people around the world."

"So, Grandpa – if you had to pick a couple things that make all these inventors so special, what would they be?" I asked.

"For one, no question that an inventor has to have vision. He or she has to foresee a need for something of value to people, and a way to make it become a reality. Assuming he has the right spark to bring energy and focus around it, it becomes his dream. Then, once focused, he has to have the drive to keep pushing an idea un- til all of the obstacles have been overcome. Somewhere along the way, inspiration may help to make it all a reality."

We both thought about that for a minute, Grandpa chewing his lower lip and gazing at something I couldn't see. "I think I have those qualities, at least most of the time. But maybe they're not as refined in me, and maybe I'm waiting for my inspiration."

"But what if an inventor doesn't have all those qualities?" I wondered out loud. "What if he has only ideas, and he wants to be a Mr. Thermostat, or a Ms. Scotchgard, or whatever, but he has no ability to pull it off? Doesn't he need some help along the way?"

"You're absolutely right," Grandpa replied. "I look at it as having three phases – first there's the vision, dream, or idea. Then there's turning it into a product – I guess some people would call that execution. Finally, there's how to connect with the people who need it – some would call that commercialization. Even Edison said not to waste your time inventing something that people don't really need."

"You see, Grandpa," I reflected, "sometimes I think I have ideas, but I don't have anything else needed to go with it. It seems like my dad is always putting me down for my poor ability to execute, and that takes away from any decent ideas I may have. He says I should just concentrate on English and literature – stay away from the other more scientific stuff."

"You mentioned that before. Believe me, I'm all ears when it comes to ideas," said Grandpa. "That's just terrific that you've got some ideas clanking around in that head of yours. Come on now, tell me more."

"Well, we have these three aquariums at home. Dad has two

44

55-gallon tanks – one fresh, the other salt water. Then this last Christmas, I got a new 35-gallon setup of my own. Do you know how much work it is to keep a fish tank clean—let alone three huge ones? Even though we have some good power filters, there's water changes and gravel and glass cleaning that has to be done all the time. Unfortunately, I'm the one stuck with most of the work. I was thinking that if someone could come up with a more powerful gravel cleaner – that would be awesome. There are squeeze-bulb-type vacuum tubes and vacuum siphons that connect to your faucet, but either they're too much work, or they get plugged up, or they drain too much water. There's gotta be something better out there. And if there isn't..." my voice trailed off, but I don't think Grandpa missed my optimism.

"Wow, this is super – you've got an idea there," exclaimed Grandpa. "Let me find my pad and we can start sketching something out on a piece of paper." With that, Grandpa made his way to a drawer. He had more energy in his step than I had noticed all weekend. Pushing aside a bunch of junk, he pulled out a yellow legal pad.

As he fumbled for a pencil, he thought out loud. "So it sounds like you need a motor connected to an impeller for suction, connected to a large capacity filter, connected to a large tube that would act like a vacuum cleaner and tumble the gravel. Does that sound like it would cover the things you're looking to do?" he asked as he tossed me a pencil.

"Yeah, I think so. And we'll need to design it to hang on the side of the glass, but only temporarily, while you're using it." Grandpa started to sketch my idea out right there on the kitchen table. In the meantime, my jaw was doing quite the number on the gum in my mouth, chomping on it mercilessly in anticipation as I watched my idea come to life on the sketch pad.

"So, Josh, you show me what the vacuum tube would look like," he invited.

I sketched that out, and for the first time found myself wishing I had paid better attention in art class. "I'll need your help, though, with how the impeller, motor, and filter would all work together," I told him.

"No problem, we'll figure something out," he said. "Let's see, because we don't want to have to prime the pump, the impeller will have to reach down far enough into the water as it hangs on the side glass." He quickly sketched what might be a viable configuration. "So," he went on, "what do you suppose we'll need to do to stop this from plugging up too quickly, like the other products do?"

"Well, I suppose we'll need a larger filter," I said.

"Right, but because we have limited space to get into the tank past the flip-up cover, we'll need to make it flat, with a decent amount of surface area for the foam filter pad. How about something that looks like this?" He continued with purposeful pencil strokes, only occasionally needing the eraser end. "Now, if we put a nice motor on top of all this, maybe we've got something. We can play with the actual size as we go along, but I'll just put some rough dimensions on the basic components like this, and...."

"Ta da!" He held up the pad with his design. It was no Rembrandt, but maybe Leonardo daVinci would have been proud. After all, I thought to myself, he was not only an artist, but also an inventor. Wasn't he the guy who designed flying machines and armored cars hundreds of years ago?

"Now let's go build it!" said Grandpa. He was practically bouncing on his heels with excitement.

"What? Build it? Right now? How are we going to do that?"

"Josh, Josh, Josh, my boy." He shook his head and smiled at me. "Don't you know what workshops are for? I've been working on my invention all this time; now let's give yours a mighty swing. I've got a lathe, a bandsaw, and a drill press out there. You know I'm a pack rat – I've collected all sorts of odd stuff over the years. Let's see what we can find."

"I can't believe it! We're actually going to try to bring my idea to life?" I asked. Memories of conversations with my dad flashed into my mind. That was certainly not anything I would have been saying to him. I was anxious to get started, but it was well past lunchtime and my stomach was growling big time. "I'm going to quickly grab a few things for us to snack on," I said. Besides, I thought to myself, what about poor Sally? I think she must be hungry too.

"Sure," said Grandpa, "but food is secondary to this – we have no time to waste."

Chapter Five

The Prototype

"I have been impressed with the urgency of doing. Knowing is not enough; we must apply. Being willing is not enough; we must do."
— *Leonardo da Vinci, 15th-century Italian artist and inventor*

"So, Josh, have you heard of the concept of a prototype?" Grandpa asked as we made our way into the workshop.

"I have an idea what it means, but you tell me," I said, somewhat distracted by that familiar oil and straw smell I had earlier gotten a whiff of at the window.

"In effect, you're building a working model to prove out a concept. It won't necessarily look anything like what a finished product would. You just need to figure out if it has a chance of working. The big question is, can we find enough stuff – no matter how ugly – to make a working prototype. Let me show you to my storage closet – we'll see. Right this way, my young inventor."

The word – inventor – had such a nice ring to it, but I was certainly not yet worthy. Maybe I could now be considered a tinkerer, I thought, as we headed toward the corner of the building. Just then I noticed we were passing right by what I presumed was

Grandpa's hitch invention. "So, Grandpa, aren't you even going to show me your invention?" I asked.

"Not today, Grandson. I had my chance yesterday. I'll be much prouder and happier to show it off to you when it works. There's only one horse in this race today. Let's focus on your project and not get distracted. We've got a lot to do before you leave."

Grandpa proceeded to open the door to a long walk-in closet with three shelves on each side. The shelves were brimming with every type of gadget and piece of material you could imagine – not in any particular order, but I was pretty sure Grandpa would know where to find most anything. Some people might call it a graveyard of junk. I'm sure in Grandpa's eyes it was a trove of fine treasure.

"Let's see," he said. "We're going to need some plastic blocks and sheets, a small motor, a cord with plug, some tubing, some foam, and an intake tube." With that, he started to pick out some pieces that might work. "Great – I think this motor might just do the trick. This tube for the vacuum pick up might be a bit too small in diameter, but let's give it a go." He had proved my hunch right – he had found enough to cobble together a prototype.

"We'll need to turn some plastic parts on the lathe for the adapters and impeller," he said, "and there'll be some bandsaw work for the filter plate. Let's crank up the old machines." I watched as Grandpa inserted a block of plastic into the lathe spindle – something I'm sure he could do blindfolded. With a flip of a switch, the motor started to rev up, and my heartbeat went right along with it, pounding harder with excitement at each beat.

"While I do the lathe work," Grandpa said, "you can go outside and round up some gravel – the closest thing you can find to aquarium gravel. There're some buckets over there and a screen in the closet you can use to filter out the particles that are too fine."

I headed out to find some gravel to use with our prototype. By the driveway I located some that might work. Leaning over the bucket with the screen on top, I piled some gravel on and started a back-and-forth sifting motion. Sally had followed me and was watching intently. Dogs always seem to be curious when you do something new and weird. I wondered if this was the way the gold panhandlers did it way back in the last century. Who knows – maybe this invention would turn into my own pot of gold? Crazy thinking, but at least I was thinking, and seemingly so was Sally.

I returned to the workshop to find that Grandpa had already finished the first part. He was wiping his brow with a shop rag in one hand while in the other he held the finished part, the impeller base. He was holding it out, admiring it. "Here, Josh, take this and run some sandpaper over it to smooth it out," he said while handing it over and pointing to the sandpaper on the workbench. "That reminds me – while you're sanding, I want to tell you the story of waterproof sandpaper. Mr. Francis Okie was an ink maker who invented the product after noticing that his manufacturing neighbor was always struggling with the dust and fire hazards of dry sanding. Mr. Okie ordered some minerals from 3M to experiment with. The top guy at 3M, Mr. William McKnight, happened to notice the request come through, and he was so intrigued by the idea that he contacted Mr. Okie. Long story short, McKnight ended up hiring him, and they got together to make 3M's first really unique and patentable product, Wet/Dry sandpaper."

As he worked, Grandpa continued with details about another key 3M inventor, Mr. Richard Drew. "He's considered the father of Scotch brand self-adhesive tapes, both masking and cellophane," he said. "It's hard to believe there are now more than 600 varieties of tape on the market. Mr. Drew is also in the National Inventors Hall of Fame."

And so it was that we continued to work on my idea for an aquarium gravel cleaner. Grandpa kept busy with all of the machining – the turning, drilling, and cutting needed for the various mechanical parts. And then, as to be expected, there was some re-turning, re-drilling, and re-cutting. Those trusty old machines whirred and purred with no more complaint than an occasional drop of oil or a shave of plastic volleyed in our direction. Grandpa kept me off the machines, but I assisted with the other stuff until we had some things ready to put together. Oh yeah, we used plenty of screws and, of course, 3M glue, but I can personally guarantee that we did not use one piece of duct tape. I think Sally could vouch for that as well, as she was attentively watching all the unexpected activity.

I was amazed at how Grandpa could continue to work hard while at the same time rattling off details about more of Minnesota's great inventors. As I was a captive listener, he wasn't about to let that opportunity go by. Even the riding lawnmower sitting in the corner reminded him of the engineer who had developed many of Toro's industry-leading innovations. I heard how Mr. Richard Thorud came up with improvements to enhance the safety and efficiency of mowers and snow blowers, while making them more environmentally friendly.

Finally, at 8:23 that night, after a short break for a light dinner, the awaited moment had come. We were ready to try out the gravel-cleaning device.

"Run back into the house and fill up the washtub in the laundry room," Grandpa said. "Then dump that gravel in there." Grandpa followed at a slower gait, cradling my baby in his arm as he made his way from the workshop.

We both watched as the gravel made its way to the bottom of the tub, swirling from the force of the flow of water from the faucet. Grandpa hung the device on the side of the tub, and we waited for the gravel to settle and the tub to fill. He plugged one end of the tubing into the filter plate and handed me the other end – the vacuum intake tube. He proceeded to plug the motor into the electrical outlet. The impeller churned and whirred in the water, expelling a bunch of bubbles while creating suction – a good sign.

"Okay," he said. "Now start vacuuming up that gravel."

I carefully dipped the tube into the gravel, kind of like when you first do a check with your toe from the dock at the lake.

"Don't be so shy," said Grandpa. "Dig it right in there."

I did as he said, and the gravel was sucked right up into the tube, climbing quickly. I pulled the tube up so that the gravel would fall right back down, but I wasn't quite quick enough. It had completely filled the tube. Damn! Soon we were hearing sharp pinging sounds, and the next thing we knew, the impeller had seized up. Then the motor stopped. Good news – I failed!

I gave Grandpa a look that said "uh-oh." As he hurried over to unplug the motor, he called, "Don't get too uptight, Josh. This isn't the end of the world. As Mr. Bakken would say, we're on our way to success."

"What?" I said in disbelief. "The frigging thing froze up on us!"

"Yes, I know, Josh, but the important thing is for us to understand why. This is not rocket science – there's just a critical balance between some of the components that needs to be adjusted. The motor may be a bit too powerful, the intake tube probably needs to have a bigger diameter, the foam needs to be denser, and we need a safety guard in front of the impeller to prevent tiny particles from jamming it up. When we have some time, we can play with all of those pieces to come up with something that will probably work."

"Really? You think we can make it work?"

"It's got great promise," said Grandpa. "This is only our first attempt – there might be many more prototypes after this. In fact, you should really name this one, so that we can name each version that comes after it."

"Alright," I said, thinking for a few seconds. "Let's name this one the *Red Wag 1,* after my favorite fish."

"Okay, sounds good," said Grandpa. "Now for the next one, we're going to need some help getting the right materials. Maybe your dad, with all of his contacts in industry, can locate the right things. The density of that filter pad, for one thing, is going to be critical."

"Oh, I don't know if Dad will be much interested in helping. I told you it feels like he's written me off for anything that has to do with math or science. One time when I asked him about the sum of the square of two sides of an isosceles triangle, his eyes just glazed over like he was too tired to deal with it. He already told me to count him out for any future science projects after getting so embarrassed at the science fair a few years back."

"Really? What happened?"

"Well, it's a long story. I made this demonstration of a volcano. I had a three-dimensional cutaway to illustrate how the pressure of the lava builds up underneath. I had connected a squeeze bottle to a tube to make the lava flow up and out, with some troughs around the sides to catch it. Well, I had talked my Dad into taking the afternoon off from work to come check it out. Let's just say he should probably have stayed at work."

"Oh no," Grandpa winced. "What happened?"

"Well, my dad was talking to me about it when one of the judges comes by to score it. She was leaning over it, really studying it quite carefully. So I go to demonstrate the lava flow, but in my excitement to show it off, I squeezed just a bit too hard on the lava bottle."

"And?" Did I see Grandpa's mouth twitching just a bit at the corners? Well, I guess I could see the humor in this too.

"I was the one who had insisted to Dad that we use ketchup for the lava. It seemed to have the closest consistency and color. It hit her square on the front of her white shirt."

"Ouch!"

"Needless to say, I was not an award winner that afternoon. And Dad," I said with emphasis, "was in a crabby mood all the way home."

Chapter Six

The Medical Legacy

*"Our greatest weakness lies in giving up. The most certain way
to succeed is always to try just one more time."*
—*Thomas A. Edison, America's most prolific inventor,
with 1,093 patents*

Contrary to my nature, I made a point of setting the alarm so I could get up early Sunday morning and be responsible for breakfast. I figured I owed it to Grandpa. He had worked awfully hard all day Saturday, especially considering how it came right on top of everything that happened on Friday. He was really dragging as he came wandering into the kitchen.

"How are you doing this morning, Grandpa?"

"Doing okay Josh, thanks. That was quite the full day yesterday. I'm hoping I can relax a bit today."

"Well, I'll make you some breakfast, but this time we're going low cholesterol – just cereal, a banana, and some toast. May not taste as good as yours, but then you'll get all that great food this afternoon to make up for it."

"Oh, that will be fine," he replied.

I sat down at the table across from him and cleared my throat. "So, Grandpa, I've got a lot of mixed emotions about yesterday. I'm excited that we were able to come up with a prototype of my idea so quickly, but I feel bad that you're still stuck on yours. Why was mine so easy while yours is not?"

Grandpa was slicing a banana into his bowl of corn flakes. He paused to consider my question. "Well, mine is a bit more complicated. My idea was more of a stretch in the first place, and of course executing it has been a challenge. Your idea, on the other hand, was just a logical extension of some basic filtration principles. A lot of inventions like yours are just a matter of making other things do a better job. Some are really simple ideas." He set the banana peel aside and wiped his hands. "One that jumps to mind has to do with your ordinary everyday shopping bags – why not put handles on them? Mr. Walter Deubener and his wife came up with that idea, and, of course, it was an immediate hit. Another example is the Breathe Right strip used to help nasal congestion and prevent snoring, invented by Mr. Bruce Johnson. It's a very simple concept to keep your nostrils open by pulling from the outside, but nobody ever thought of it before, or figured out how to do it."

I smiled as I remembered a *Saturday Night Live* spoof of the Breathe Right commercials. It involved a much larger strip – one designed for butt cheeks, not noses. I couldn't stop laughing after I saw that.

"Y'know," continued Grandpa, "those nose strips didn't really take off until some NFL players started wearing them. Just goes to show you, at the end of the day, the big question is whether you can make a product at an attractive price and then successfully market it. You can have the greatest idea in the world, but if nobody even knows about it, or can use it, or wants to buy it, what have you gained?"

"Why do inventors have this compelling need to invent? Is it because they all want to get rich?" I queried.

"I suppose that's part of it for some inventors – the Great American Dream, you know. But I think a lot of it is just the satisfaction of coming up with something that improves other people's quality of life. And if you think maybe you have that gift, and a dream to make it happen, then you don't want to let it go to waste."

"Come to mention it," I added, "Friday night, after your heart episode, and you had made tracks to your bedroom early, I was worrying about you and I started to think about pacemakers a lot. So I hopped on the computer and did a little research. I found out that when Earl Bakken was a young man, he and his brother-in-law started in a garage, just like you and so many inventors. Along the way his company had a lot of ups and downs, and he was forced into becoming a businessman when his heart was only into inventing. Bottom line, though, is that his goal all along has been to help people. He followed his early pastor's advice and spent a lifetime serving his fellow man – inventing instruments that reduce pain, restore health, and extend life.

"Then the other cool thing I read is that Mr. Bakken recognized that there is much more to health than medical devices. He thinks that patients who get care from compassionate and caring doctors do much better, and there is a connection between the mind and the body, and how a patient heals."

"Yes, that's such a wonderful view of things, and it is all a great story." Grandpa smiled at me, and I could tell he was pleased that I was taking such an interest in the subject. "We could talk about this all day, but, you know what, we've got to get packed up to get to church. We had better load up the truck with the corn and the tables and chairs and get going. I wouldn't want to be late for my tribute." He winked at me.

"Tribute? I didn't know about any tribute. What's that all about?"

"Oh, didn't your dad tell you? They're doing a little program for me today – I had mentioned that to him on the phone. They're honoring me for my 30 years as an elder on the church board. I've decided to step down, and they wanted to give me a tribute. So we can't be late."

"Awesome," I said. I wondered why Dad hadn't mentioned it. "Let's get going."

Grandpa climbed up into the bed of his pickup so I could do all the lifting of the chairs, tables, and corn. Sally pranced around with the expectation of going along, but she had to be content with gazing longingly after us as we pulled out. As we turned onto the main road, I began to reflect about Mr. Bakken. His story prompted me to ask about other great Minnesota medical contributors.

Grandpa had no problem answering. "Mr. Bakken got a lot of his inspiration and guidance from Dr. C. Walton Lillehei, a cardiac surgeon at the University of Minnesota who was known around the world. Dr. Lillehei is considered one of the founders of open heart surgery, coming up with things like heart valves and improvements to the heart-lung machine. He later was one of a small group of surgeons who performed human heart transplants." I barely had time to be impressed by Grandpa's vast breadth of knowledge before he was off and running again.

"Going back further, Lillehei was a protégé of Dr. Owen Wangensteen – I love the guy because he had his roots in farming. But he also became a well-known university surgeon and innovator. His best known invention goes back to the '30s when the Wangensteen gastric suction system was used to aspirate gas and fluid from the stomach and intestines. Wouldn't you know, he didn't even bother to patent it – he wasn't interested in protecting his inventions for personal gain."

I couldn't stop thinking of the name. How awesome! What better name to have for a medical device – the "Wangensteen system." I loved it – it sounded like the utmost of medical designs. I thought that if I were a patient, I'd want the doctors telling my parents, "We used the Wangensteen system on your son, and he's coming around just fine." They'd head home happy, that's for sure.

"Thinking about those three guys," I said, "it seems like they all were connected in a way. One became the mentor for the next, and so forth. The younger person becomes the protégé. Is that the way it typically works?" I asked.

"That's often the case, especially in the field of medicine. So much knowledge gets transferred, but each new person brings his or her own talent to help solve a new problem."

"What other big medical contributions have been made by Minnesotans?"

"Well, another great medical inventor is Dr. Henry Buchwald. He has done great work coming up with a way to reduce cholesterol levels, as well as developing devices like the world's first infusion port and an implantable infusion pump for delivering drugs throughout the body.

"Then there's Professor Robert Vince from the University of Minnesota – he's what they call a medicinal chemist. Mr. Vince is on the leading edge of some new antiviral drugs. His team has already come up with the most effective drug treatment for treating herpes. But there's another drug that could have an even bigger impact that's been proven successful in the lab. For the last ten years he's been working on an exciting new drug to fight HIV. The University patented it and has licensed it to GlaxoSmithKline. They're expecting FDA approval any day now. If that one comes through, it will be really huge – most importantly because of the lives saved, but an added benefit is that the university will get big royalties that can be re-invested in more research capability.

"Finally, we can't forget the contributions of Mr. Carl Oja, who designed devices to improve the lives of invalids and injured people. His four-footed cane and "Spine Guard" stretcher products have been of great value. A football fan like you – you've probably watched one used at a game when an injured player was carried off the field, but didn't realize it."

We were pulling into the church parking lot. I reflected about all those medical contributors – what great examples of inventors wanting to improve the quality of life of their fellow man! I knew one thing: If it weren't for a pacemaker and a pill, my grandpa might not be driving me to church right now.

I looked forward to more good conversation with Grandpa and, of course, a day of good chow. To be honest, at that particular moment it was a near toss-up as to which was more important, but with each minute that passed, food was gaining an edge.

Chapter Seven

Church & the Greatest Generation

"They came of age during the Great Depression and the Second World War and went on to build modern America – men and women whose everyday lives of duty, honor, achievement, and courage gave us the world we have today."
—Tom Brokaw, newscaster

Chapter Seven – Church & the Greatest Generation

It was about 10:20 on this last Sunday of August, and a number of people were already arriving at church for the 11:00 service. Families were tumbling out of cars, greeted by a beautiful breezy morn; some were stepping out a bit more carefully, laden with dishes of various shapes and form. Several guys were setting up their grills in the parking lot for the hamburgers and hot dogs. We unloaded the corn and tables, and I was tasked with retrieving the large pots from the kitchen for boiling the corn. There were a number of people milling about in the kitchen, but only one recognized me right away.

"Well hello there," said Emily Ferguson – she had been a family friend going way back. "Good to see you, Josh – you've grown a bit." I grinned, embarrassed, as she went on. "What has it been – almost a year? Is the rest of your family here?"

"Hi, Mrs. Ferguson," I replied. "No, it's just me down for a weekend visit. You're right, it has been about a year."

"What brings you down?" she asked.

"Just checking up on Grandpa Ralph. I'm really glad I came down. He just told me about the tribute to him at church today." Remembering what I was tasked to do, I continued, "Say, can you tell me where they keep the big pots for the corn?"

"They're in the back room – I'll show you." As we walked toward the storage pantry, she said, "Yes, the tribute to your Grandpa is well deserved. He's done so much to keep this church on track and flourishing. There are the pots," she pointed out. "We'll probably see you later at the potluck."

"Okay – see ya. I'm looking forward to some great food."

As I headed back up, a few others gave me a "Hi, Josh," or at least a friendly smile. Back outside, a small crowd had gathered around my grandpa, shaking hands or back patting. I sidled into the group, and Grandpa reminded everyone who I was. That generated a lot more hellos and how ya' doin's. There's something about the community feeling you get from a smaller country church as opposed to what I was used to at home. Even for someone who was just a visitor, I felt very welcome and comfortable.

I wasn't quite so comfortable once the service began, however, because I could sense Grandpa's nervousness. I've never known him to seek out the spotlight, and he knew he was about to be summoned to the front. As he strode up the aisle and took his place next to the pastor, I couldn't help but empathize.

Early in the service, the pastor gave a wonderful tribute, giving example after example of contributions he had made, and of course thanking him on behalf of the entire congregation. I'm guessing Grandpa must have overcome any aversion to the spotlight pretty quickly after all that. Pride welled up in me, and I deeply wished my parents could have been there. My mom would have been so proud of her father. With a flush to his face and a bounce to his step, Grandpa came sauntering back to his seat.

I couldn't believe my ears once the pastor started in on his sermon. Wouldn't you know, it was about the parable of the five talents, in which various servants were given different amounts of money by their master according to their abilities. Some prospered; others did not. I wondered about myself and Grandpa. Were we using our abilities in the right way? My mind wandered, thinking of what had been transpiring all weekend.

After the service, everyone scurried to get their food out for the potluck. Soon the long row of tables was teeming with colorful dishes. In addition to the chicken and meats, there were chips and salads of all varieties, buns and breads, and of course a great selection of cakes, cookies, and pies for dessert. Some of the guys, who had quickly fired up their grills, began to plop hamburgers and wieners on hot, welcoming grates. It wouldn't be long before those juicy, charred slabs would be transferred to even more welcoming plates.

"That was a nice tribute they gave you, huh, Grandpa?"

"Yeah, I'll say. I had forgotten about a number of things the pastor mentioned. He did a nice job, but I am just one of many." I could tell Grandpa wasn't comfortable with all the attention, because he quickly changed the subject, telling me to make sure to get in line early to grab a piece of fried chicken before it ran out. While others got his attention with more handshakes and back-slapping, I decided to make a dash for the food line.

My plate was soon piled high with a variety of almost everything. I carefully balanced it, taking special care to watch two pieces of that prized chicken. I headed for an empty table.

Saving a spot for Grandpa, I sat down to dig in. It wasn't long before an elderly couple who looked somewhat familiar stopped and asked if they could take two of the empty chairs. Great. It looked as though I was cornered by a couple of old folks who wanted to talk. I smiled politely and said, "Sure," as I tried to remember who they were. Fortunately, they made it easy for me.

"You're, Josh, right? Not sure if you remember us, but we're Bob and Rene Wilson – good friends of your grandpa going back to when we were kids," said Bob. "We used to do a lot of things with your grandma and grandpa over the years. Boy, I'll tell you, he was a lifesaver for us last January. It was late on a Saturday night, and our furnace gave out on us. It was about 25 degrees below zero, and your Grandpa didn't hesitate to come over to fix it. He just knows an awful lot about everything, and he's always willing to drop whatever he's doing to help."

"Yes, I know," I said. "I've been hearing a lot, and of course getting quite the education this weekend about all the Minnesota inventors he admires so much. You must know he's been trying to come up with something of his own, too, and I'm confident he will – at least someday."

"Yes, he's mentioned it," said Bob, "but he won't tell us what it is. Of course, he's shooting to win an award at June's convention. From what I hear he'll be up against some real pros who are working on some new things, though."

"Yeah, you may be right." I was tempted to tell them about Grandpa's incident and my prototype, but then decided not to share all the details of our weekend. Good thing, because out of the corner of my eye I spotted Grandpa making his way over to our table.

"How are you doing, Bob and Rene?" Grandpa greeted them warmly. "I see you've hooked up with my grandson," he said, sitting down between us.

"Yep, we were just starting to chow down and have a chat with him," Rene said. "As you can see, we weren't too bashful filling up our plates, but then I don't imagine anyone was."

"Grandpa – I knew you'd be late getting in line, so I saved you this piece of chicken." I tried to maneuver it deftly to his plate, but I kind of fumbled the hand-off and it slipped off my fork. I guess quarterback isn't my position, either. I don't think he minded, though, that it landed with a splat in the middle of his potato salad, where he quickly recovered it.

"Thanks – super," he said. "Here, we can trade. I brought you this piece of fresh blueberry pie – I remembered that's one of your favorites, and there was only one piece left."

"Sweet – thanks, Grandpa."

"So Josh," he went on, "you and I have shared a lot about inventors the last couple days. Along those lines, Bob and I have shared a lot of war stories. He lost an older brother in World War II."

"Yes, my brother, Bill, died late in the war," said Bob. "His ship sank in the Pacific, not too long after Ralph lost his older brother. I think that's why we have developed such a bond."

"Oh, sorry to hear that," I mumbled on the surface, while my mind was quickly doing a deep, deep dive. Was I supposed to know that Grandpa had an older brother who died in the war? Was I told that at some time and had just forgotten? I searched the depths of my memory, but found no treasure of an answer.

Bob continued, "I think back, and that really was the Greatest Generation. I guess us three old folks here, even though we were younger than the soldiers at the time, have snuck in under that generation line too. We can call ourselves great – in my mind, anyway."

"I don't think you'd have any argument," I said. "I do know about Tom Brokaw's book, *The Greatest Generation*, even though I haven't read it yet."

"Well, I just finished reading it," said Bob. "It's a wonderful book – kind of a compilation of stories and wisdom from our generation. Many of us lived through the Great Depression and then were supremely challenged during World War II. But we were dedicated, hard workers and survived to make a better world."

"Yes, Josh, the war years were when some real inventing took place under extraordinary circumstances," said Grandpa. "The inventors during that period really had their backs against the wall, time-wise. They didn't have the luxury of tinkering around, like I do. They consistently came up with super inventions in a matter of months, if not weeks. The key is they were able to focus on a goal, and then get it done. And they didn't have the advantage of the fancy software tools we have today, like CAD/CAM. In my mind, they moved the unmovable; they solved the unsolvable; they achieved the unachievable." Emotion was starting to take over my grandpa's voice. "One of the main reasons we won the war," he went on, "is because the United States was able to rapidly mobilize to meet the threats from Germany and Japan with new and improved technology. Complete industries were turned upside down to meet President Roosevelt's challenge to overwhelmingly outproduce the enemy. Believe it or not, after 1941, only 139 cars were built during the entire war because car manufacturers were so busy making airplanes and airplane parts."

"From my perspective," interjected Bob, "just knowing people were helping on the home front made it a little bit easier to come to terms with the tragedies we heard about on a daily basis occurring overseas. That people here valued soldiers like my brother and were willing to do what they could for their country, well, that just really helped. That was quite a different feeling from what we experienced with Vietnam."

"What were younger guys like you and Grandpa doing during the war?" I asked.

"Oh," Bob chuckled, remembering. "We became expert salvage collectors. Salvage collectors *extraordinaire*, I might add. We searched in alleys, ditches, anywhere, for things that might be of value for the war effort. The government wanted us to collect old tires and scrap metal that could be reused and turned into armaments. Besides, anyone who came up with 20 pounds of scrap could get in free to the local movie house in Luverne, called the *Palace*. My folks would only let me go to the Saturday matinee, though, because at night there were typically blackouts with sirens going off to warn us to shut off all lights. Even though we were 1,200 miles from either coast, we just didn't know if we'd be subject to an air attack. Wasn't that something else? That was a whole different life back then."

"Sounds like it. But I kinda like the idea of getting into that movie house. So, Grandpa, have there been any movies that have inspired you to invent?" I asked. "When I did my research on Earl Bakken, I found out that he was inspired by the movie, *Frankenstein*. He became intrigued with figuring out how to use electricity to restore life, and eventually came up with the pacemaker."

"No, I can't recall that a movie had that effect on me," he replied, "but there's always tomorrow."

"So, who were some of those Greatest Generation inventors

from Minnesota?" I asked. Now that Grandpa had started me down this path, it turned out I couldn't get enough of his stories. Who would've expected, I thought to myself.

"Well, certainly one of the most important was Dr. Robert Page," said my grandpa. "He was considered America's foremost authority on radar, which had been worked on since the '30s by both the Americans and the British. In the end, Allied supremacy on the seas was due in large part to our radar capabilities, and many historians say that even though the atomic bomb ended the war, radar won it. I've read Mr. Page's book – it was fascinating. It's amazing how, after a long period of early development, their work all came together rather rapidly as a military tool. I spent a day in the Sioux Falls library a few weeks ago. I had one of the librarians helping me dig around – she was a saint the way she helped me; bless her heart. I was trying to find out whatever happened to this great American hero. I'm still working on it."

"Well, anyway," he continued, "back to the story of the atomic bomb, you probably know from science class what an isotope is and how uranium has all kinds of isotopes, right? So the question back in 1940 was which one might split the best to create tremendous energy. Dr. Alfred Nier was Minnesota's best-known physicist, and he became actively involved with the Manhattan project, the secret code name for the development of the atomic bomb. He recommended that uranium 235 would be best suited to be made into the bomb. After a long period of secret development, finally, on August 6, 1941, the first atomic bomb was dropped on Hiroshima, Japan, from a B-29 named the *Enola Gay*. Another bomb was dropped a few days later, and not long thereafter the Japanese surrendered."

Visions of a cloud mushrooming high up into the sky flashed through my mind. I recalled seeing pictures of that, but not much about the devastation far below. There probably aren't many pictures of that. I don't imagine anyone from the daily newspaper wished they were there with a camera that day. I shuddered, thinking of the tens of thousands of men, women, and children who woke up that morning not knowing that they would meet a fiery death. And it happened twice? I am glad I didn't have to make those decisions.

Grandpa continued, "But what good would any of the bombs have been if you couldn't drop them accurately? The old hydraulic bomb bay doors opened quite slowly and put a drag on the plane. So the government put out a contract for the design of a new compressor. In the matter of a month, Mr. Richard Cornelius and his team came up with a super lightweight, high-compression air compressor that was able to open the bomb bay doors with a bang. It did other things as well, such as discharging the shells of spent munitions." Once again I was impressed by Grandpa's ability to recite this litany of facts off the top of his mind.

"Of course," continued Grandpa, "you always want to do your best to get those bombs to land in the right spot, to destroy your military targets. I remember when four hydrogen bombs were dropped by mistake over southern Spain in the '60s – all due to a midair mishap between two airplanes. One of the bombs landed in the ocean, and they had to figure out a way to retrieve it. Well, a Minnesota inventor, Mr. Harold Froehlich, had designed a miniature deep-dive research vessel called ALVIN. It was only 22 feet long and carried just a couple of people. It was pressed into emergency service."

As I began to imagine being one of those people squeezed into that cool little sub searching for a bomb off of some craggy shelf at the bottom of the ocean, Grandpa came up with an intriguing bit of additional information. "And they almost didn't make it back up," he added.

"Oh, no. What happened?" I asked.

"Well," he said, "the bomb had a parachute attached to it, and while they were working to retrieve it the parachute got in the way, completely obstructing their vision. It caused all kinds of instant panic. How would you like to be working with a hydrogen bomb thousands of feet underwater while practically blind?'

"No thanks," I said. "How did it all end up?"

"With the first try, the line snapped, and they lost the bomb. They had to find it all over again, but they were finally able to bring it to the surface, and of course were heroes for doing so."

"Quite a story," I said. I could see that Bob was enjoying the story as much as I did.

"Getting back to the wartime contributions," Grandpa continued, "automatic pilot capability was another feature the bombers benefited from. Over 30,000 of them employed a critical system invented by Mr. Willis Gille from Honeywell – the electrical controls for the auto pilot. He brought that design from conception to large-scale production in a matter of just six months.

"Then there was Mr. Herbert Dalglish, who also provided numerous inventions that helped the war effort. They included floating bridges, high-pressure valves used on Navy ships, and special couplings for pipelines that were critical to the supply of fuel during the D-Day invasion.

"Mr. John Gondek revolutionized the design of hydraulics on Navy ships during the war and came up with a unique lightweight loader for torpedo tubes. Also, just 90 days after the sunken ships were raised at Pearl Harbor, he supervised the complete reworking of their hydraulic gear.

"And we can't forget the aeronautical engineers I mentioned earlier – many of them were doing their work as part of the war effort."

"That's a lot of people," I said, looking for a break in the list of accomplishments. "How many more stories do you have?" I asked, as I finished up the last remains from my plate and reached for my fresh blueberry pie. "It seems kind of weird talking so much about war during a pleasant visit at a nice, peaceful country church on a Sunday."

"Yes, it is kind of strange, isn't it?" replied Grandpa. "What we must realize, though, is that however much we don't like war, the fact of the matter is if we had not geared up with the needed technology to meet the challenges from Germany and Japan, perhaps we wouldn't be free to go to a church like this. I'll mention just a few more people.

"You know when you look through a gun eyepiece and see crosshairs? Mr. Norman Mears came up with the commercial etching capability needed for those grids on the armament eyepieces.

"Mr. Glen Dye built machines that made it possible to process X-ray films completely automatically so that important castings, artillery shells, and propellers could be inspected easily and the bad ones could be thrown away.

"Whew – there are some others," said Grandpa, "but I'll stop after just one more little story. Remember I told you about Dr. Schmitt and his trigger switch inspired by jumping frogs? Besides contributing with his wife to the Manhattan Project, he also came up with a clever way to distract the German radar operators. He found a method to transmit jokes slightly off-channel. The story goes that when the operators listened to the jokes, they couldn't keep track of their radar signals. It fooled some of them for months.

"So that gives you an idea of the contribution of many Minnesotans to the war effort," he concluded. "And it truly was a team effort. You can talk all you want about teamwork on your football team, but there's nothing like a whole country coming together, focused on a singular goal."

"But I don't think we would have won it all if it hadn't been for Mrs. McMurty's fender," Bob said, chuckling.

"Oh, not that story," implored Renee.

Of course, that made me want to hear it. "Yes, tell me," I said.

Bob began, "Well, this goes back to when Ralph and I were kids scavenging for scrap metal. One day I overheard old man McMurty at the barber shop. He was complaining about his wife's hobby – he called it junkyard gardening. She liked to turn just about anything into a planter for flowers in the backyard. McMurty was saying that the ugliest thing she had was a turned-over front fender from a '32 Chevy that was starting to rust – he'd been trying to convince her to get rid of it. So one day my friend Ralphie over here spots some flowerpots on end-of-season clearance down at Simonson's. Negotiator that he is, he points out a bunch of scratches and scuffs, and ends up getting them all for 50 cents. We snuck out the next night and headed for McMurty's backyard. Ralph's holding a flashlight and standing guard. I'm doing the digging, transplanting the flowers. I did a great job of moving those flowers over to the pots in the dark, if I do say so myself. Turned out to be a win-win deal for everybody. Mrs. McMurty ended up a patriot for her country for her metal contribution, and we got tickets into the movie house."

"Yeah, but what about the old man?" said Grandpa. "He probably got blamed and caught hell 'til his dying day."

"Well, I caught a little hell myself trying to sneak back home that night," Bob added. "Ma kept pressing me to tell her where I had been so late. I kept telling her, 'I swear to God, you gotta believe me. I was out planting flowers for Mrs. McMurty....' Of course, I couldn't tell her any of the other details."

Not altogether comfortable with a story about their shenani-
gans, Rene appeared anxious to move on to a new topic. "You guys
have talked about a lot of contributions from the men, but let's not
forget that it was mostly women who worked in the factories to
manufacture all that stuff. Everyone was involved – the teamwork
going on was incredible. Al McIntosh used to write for the Rock
County Star Herald and kept us tuned into what all was going on.
I remember that once he wrote about a lady who used to work over
at the Worthington Creamery. She put her name and address on an
egg before putting it into the crate. Wouldn't you know she heard
back from some soldier in Italy who got it. Plus, don't forget about
all those WACs."

"Okay, I admit, I don't know this one. Who were the WACs?"
I asked.

"Stands for Women's Army Corp. A lot of people don't realize
that about 150,000 women served in the armed forces during the
war," Rene replied.

People were beginning to pack up and head home. It had been
a full afternoon of conversation and good eating. I had forgotten that my original plan was to hook up with some other guys to
maybe play some touch football or at least talk sports. I had also
almost forgotten that this was the evening when we were to head
back to Sioux Falls for the flight home. Grandpa was obviously
thinking we had better get going as well, so we started to say our
good-byes.

Chapter Eight

Change in Plans

"Dreams have a way of predicting and preceding reality."
—Earl Bakken, pacemaker inventor

As we drove back toward the farmhouse, I reflected on the dedication of all those wartime inventors. I could see how Grandpa was trying to follow the path they had paved. At least he's able to focus on his one passion, I thought. I'll bet a lot of those guys must have had to change directions to make different products immediately after the war. I wondered how those factories had geared back down to a normal life, so I posed that question to him.

"Well, it wasn't really that easy," he replied. "Fortunately, the government was able to assist some companies monetarily to ease the transition. There were still industrial and military needs for things like radar, cranes, photo-processing, and compressors. Many of the aeronautical capabilities are used still today or evolved and became useful for NASA's space programs. Some of the inventors went back to things they had previously been working on, or moved on to new products.

"For example, Mr. Dalglish retooled and became a leading lawn mower manufacturer. He also developed a bug detector for grain elevators. Mr. Cornelius developed a whole line of beer and soft drink dispensing equipment. Mr. Gondek designed a bunch of hydraulics, generators, and pumps. Mr. Mears used the metal etching technology from the war years to further develop color televisions in peacetime.

"So if you try to piece it all together," Grandpa continued, "I think it would it be fair to say that one of the few good things that came from the war was that it sped up technology development and provided a boost for inventors in the years that followed. Another example of something very valuable being pushed ahead is the mass production of penicillin, considered one of the most important developments of the century. Going into the war, the Brits and Americans knew that they'd have to treat a lot of war-injured, so scientists started to work feverishly together in a lab down in Illinois. They were trying to figure out how to produce the drug in mass quantities. Working with a fermented liquid from corn, they discovered it was an aid in increasing production of penicillin tenfold. They eventually were able to provide 300 billion units, which saved the lives of hundreds of thousands of soldiers during the war."

"I guess we can just say thanks to a lot of great innovators," I concluded. "Well, we've sure covered a lot of contributions from many people. "So how many Minnesota Hall of Fame inventors are there? How many do you think we've covered?"

"Oh, I'm not sure how many they total up to, but they go back to Mr. Willis Gille, who was the very first inducted in 1976. We've probably covered only about half of them."

"So, let's see," I said. "We've covered a lot of areas – from the planes to the fields, to medicine, to factories, to wartime – you name it. Who are some of the big hitters we haven't even talked about?"

"Where to begin?" he mused. "Oh!" He sat up a little straighter and grinned. "You'll love this. I presume you've got regular ol' underwear on today, right?"

"Yeah, briefs," I said. "Why do you ask?"

"I never know what you young people are into – or out of – these days. Mr. Franklin Chatfield was the designer behind many knitting and fabric processing machines for Munsingwear, making the company a leader in its day. Personally, I'm glad he did a lot of research on fabric shrinkage control while he was at it." Grandpa grinned at his own joke. I smiled politely, internally rolling my eyes at the cheesy joke.

"Moving on to more technical stuff," he continued, "another big area is electronics and computers. Unlike with underwear, though, I may be a bit 'generationally' challenged there.

"Anyway, Mr. Earl Masterson came up with inventions that led to the development of video cameras and cassette recorders. Later he was involved with the first Univac computer – it was only a mere 8 feet tall and weighed 30 tons! He also developed large, high-speed printers, tape drives, and storage for those big boys.

"But a real genius in the computer area was Mr. Seymour Cray. He led the creation of the first commercial supercomputer for Control Data. Those computers were perfect for doing the real number crunching required for scientific analysis – and they were super fast. Later, he built even faster ones at his own company, Cray Research. He was very tuned into the idea of staying fresh with his ideas, not getting distracted by old ones. He used to design and build sailboats as a hobby. There's a story that before he'd start a new one he would actually have a party to burn the old boat so it wouldn't sway his thinking. Can you believe that?"

"I suppose so," I replied. I had a sudden inspiration. "Hey, maybe that's what you need to do, Grandpa – start over with a fresh idea – maybe a completely new invention."

"I just may have to – but only if I really hit a dead end. I don't want to give up just because it's tough. I want to know that I've tried everything I can think of and have exhausted every angle."

I thought back about some times when I'd given up when things got tough. Maybe it was that chess game with Charlie Saunders, the "braniac" of the school. Maybe it was in geometry class. Maybe it was after geometry class when I was just trying to get up the courage to talk to Aubrey Green. But that was an area I didn't want to think about anymore, so I asked another question.

"Who are some of the others that overcame obstacles?" I queried.

"Well, take for example Mr. Edward Davis from the Iron Range. He spent practically his whole life working on the process of converting low-grade taconite into iron ore. That discovery was a huge economic benefit, not only for the state of Minnesota, but also internationally.

"And certainly you've eaten a Totino's frozen pizza or two in your life. Ms. Rose Totino and her husband started out with a small pizza shop. Her big thing was improving pizza crusts. She invented the first pizza dough suitable for freezing. Not happy with the traditional cardboard-tasting crust, she came up with the idea of frying it first, which resulted in a much improved version that she got a patent for.

"Mr. Frederick Jones, an African American inventor, had quite an amazing story. He was abandoned by both of his parents but became a self-taught engineer who eventually invented the refrigeration systems used in trucks around the world. So we can thank him for the fresh vegetables, meats, and seafood we get every day.

"Finally, to bring us up to more modern times, Mr. Robert Gilruth was the one who got the Mercury space program off the ground. That helped us catch up with the Soviets, who had launched the first orbiting satellite, the *Sputnik*. He designed the spacecraft itself and established astronaut qualification and training procedures. He later managed the Gemini program, directing a total of 25 space flights."

We had arrived back at the farm. Sally's tail wagged furiously as she greeted us after the long afternoon on her own. I helped Grandpa unload the chairs and tables. The orange sun peeked out behind clouds gathering in the western sky, and we prepared to wind down from a beautiful day.

Grandpa pulled back his sleeve and glanced at his wristwatch. "Looks like we have an hour or so before we have to head out to the airport," he said. "I thought maybe I would relax at the computer, catch up on some e-mails, and maybe do some research. I suppose there must be some football game on you'd like to watch?"

"Sure, sounds like a good idea." The thought of stretching out on the couch was more than a little appealing. I was feeling kind of sleepy after that big meal. "What are you researching?" I asked Grandpa.

"Do you recall what I told you about Robert Page and his work with radar? I've really been finding a lot more good information about him. It has me so intrigued, I want to keep pursuing it. It's really quite a story – the Americans, the British, and even the Germans were all racing to get it all figured out going into the war."

"Great, you do that. I'm going to run upstairs and pack first. Then I'll come back down and turn on the game," I said.

I quickly packed, and about a half hour later I began to doze off on the couch, having trouble staying tuned into the not-so-exciting game. But then I was suddenly startled by a shout from Grandpa, waking me from my stupor.

"Oh, my God!" he exclaimed. "I don't believe it! You know that great librarian at the Sioux Falls library I was telling you about – the one who was helping me research Mr. Robert Page? There's an e-mail here from her. She hooked up with some other librarians in the Twin Cities, and they've found some personal records showing family connections. Looks like Mr. Page still has a niece in the Twin Cities. There are a couple different numbers here. I think we still have some time before heading to the airport. Maybe we'll get some real gems of information. Should I try giving them a shot?"

"You mean you may have her home number? Terrific. Why don't you call right now?"

"Well, I'm no fan of invading people's privacy, but she can always just hang up."

"I'd go for it," I said, as I moved closer so I could eavesdrop on the call. Grandpa started dialing.

The first two numbers proved unsuccessful. Then I heard him hit pay dirt: "Good afternoon, is this the niece of Robert Page? It is? Wonderful!" he said. "I hope you're having a nice Sunday afternoon, and I'm sorry if I'm disrupting it. You don't know me, but my name is Ralph Lindstrom from Luverne, Minnesota. I'm wondering if I might have a few minutes of your time to discuss some research I am doing on your uncle. I consider him to be a great American hero – I so admire his accomplishments. Maybe you can help me fill in a few holes in my information." A look of disappointment crossed his face. "I see. You don't remember many of the details." He covered the mouthpiece with one hand and whispered to me, "She sounds really old." Of course, anyone older than him was considered "really old."

"Pardon me?" he continued, and repeated what she said so I

could hear. "You say I could try to talk with him, but he's in his 90s and can't communicate well? It would be better in person?" He looked astounded at what she was saying. "Well, I'd love to meet with him for a short time. Where is he located?"

It sounded as if she were willing to provide the details of his whereabouts – I could hardly believe it was this easy, either. I decided to just wait until the call was over and then get the complete scoop.

A few minutes later, Grandpa came over with the most upbeat face I had ever seen on him. He was absolutely beaming – a far cry from the face I had seen on him just Friday. He explained the details of the conversation.

"As it turns out, Mr. Page is in a nursing home in Rochester. He's there because he goes weekly to the Mayo Clinic as part of some special rehab program for stroke victims that they're trying out with him."

"So what are you thinking, Grandpa?" He didn't immediately answer.

"You know me, Josh," he finally replied. "I'm always one to strike while the iron's hot. Who knows how much longer this treasure of an American will be alive? I want to go to Rochester tomorrow. It's only about a three-hour drive, virtually all freeway."

"Well, first you have to get me to the airport tonight, right?"

"That's up to you, but this may be a chance of a lifetime. I'd love to have you come with me – school doesn't start till after Labor Day, right? When we're done, I can bring you to the bus station in Rochester and you can take a bus home – it's less than two hours. Your dad can pick you up at the bus station tomorrow instead of at the airport tonight."

The thoughts were bouncing back and forth in my head. This was indeed a great opportunity and would be a crowning finale to my weekend. But on the other hand, it could turn out to be just a very long drive to see someone who might not be that anxious to visit with us. I would also lose another day to go to the State Fair with my friends. But then, no – this really is a no brainer, I thought, as some sense started to take over. How could I possibly give up such an opportunity? In the end, thinking about the agony of my flight here had more than a little to do with finally sealing the deal.

"Count me in," I said. "I'll give my folks a call with the new plans and timeline – I imagine they'll be quite surprised. Then, if they're okay with it, I'll call the airline to cancel my reservation. When do we leave in the morning?"

"Be packed and ready to go by, let's see, make that 7:45 a.m. sharp! I'm really excited that we can do this together. That reminds me, though; I have to call Bert Sanders to say I won't be over on Monday to help him – he'll just have to wait another day."

"So getting back to this Mr. Page that we're going to try to hook up with tomorrow," I resumed. "It sounds as if his work really had an impact on history, didn't it? In fact, all those wartime inventors we discussed had such a great impact on the course of world events. If there is one thing you've taught me, it's that not only do we need to think about the benefits that inventions contribute to our daily lives, we also have to consider how they may have changed history."

"Absolutely," he replied. "And that goes back through the centuries. Most people have no idea how inventions may have actually created tipping points in history. Take Abraham Lincoln, for example. Nobody ever thinks about him as an inventor. But he was our only president who was actually issued a patent. It was for a floatation device for boats. That was immaterial, but the point is that he used his inventive mind to encourage development of a couple of critical things: the *Merrimac,* the steel-clad ship that was victorious over the *Monitor* in a key naval battle in the Civil War, and a newly designed repeating rifle. The use of 20,000 of those rifles proved to be highly advantageous in battle, certainly helping the Union to win the war."

I had learned a lot about Abraham Lincoln in school, but I never fathomed that he had an inventive mind, or even had a patent. I thought back to the story of the *Merrimac.* Even though the *Monitor* was so nimble, in the end it was the steel-clad shell of the Union boat that saved the day.

"Interesting," I said, and paused to reflect further. The discussion of history made me think about how everyone experiences some inventions that cause major changes in their lives. "So, Grandpa," I asked, "when you think back on your lifetime, what invention really stands out for you? Which one made you say,

Change in Plans

'wow' at the time?"

"Well, I guess I would have to say the television. Although it was invented in the '30s, it didn't really take off until after the war, when people settled down to a normal lifestyle and could afford them. As for color television – that didn't come along until 1953, when I was even a bit older than you are now. What about for you?"

"Gee, the personal computer and the Internet were well established by the time I was first able to take advantage of them, but use of cell phones has only just become widespread the last few years. I'd say it would have to be the cell phone."

It had been some good conversation. Wanting to be prepared for the early start, we decided to each do our own thing the rest of the evening. I headed up to bed at about 10:30. I had no sooner fallen asleep when I was awoken by some rumblings from the ceiling of my bedroom. What could that be? I thought. Squirrels already looking for a home for a cold fall and winter? A bit early for that. Maybe a bat? Then I noticed the light shining through the crack under my door. I ventured into the hall and saw the ladder from the attic pulled down in the middle of the hallway.

"Grandpa, you up there?" I called out. "What are you doing up in the attic past 11:00 at night? I hope you're not chasing some bat."

"Oh, no – I'm looking for something," he shouted back. It reminded me of the many times I had told my parents, *'nothing,'* when they asked what I was doing. You know darn well you could be more specific, but in fact you don't want the asker to really know *anything*. I decided to leave it at that, and I went back to bed. But it took awhile to get back to sleep, as I wondered what he could possibly be looking for before our trip.

Chapter Nine

The Trip

*"Joy can be real only if people look on their life as service,
and have a definite object in life outside themselves and
their personal happiness."*
—Count Leo Tolstoy, Russian author

I just don't think a 14-year-old waking up early four days in a row is part of God's natural order of things. It's just not supposed to happen. At least that's what my inner voice had been telling me since the last time I pushed the snooze alarm. But now I was hearing Grandpa's voice from downstairs. "Josh, are you up? It's awfully quiet up there – better get in gear." I guess things must be getting serious.

I dragged myself out of bed and headed to the bathroom. A quick shower, a few more things thrown into my duffel bag for the trip home, and I was headed downstairs for breakfast. We made it simple – just some toast, juice, and coffee – as we were focused on getting underway.

"Say, Grandpa – I want to bring *Red Wag 1* with me to show my folks. Is there a box out in the workshop I can put it in?"

"Yep, of course," he said. "But keep in mind it deserves a nice box, not just any old piece of corrugated."

"Right on," I said, and headed out. I made my way to the workshop and spotted a stack of boxes in a corner. Many of them were beat up or had ugly labels on them. I cast those aside and rummaged around until I found one about the right size with no labels or markings. I grabbed a shop cloth and dusted it off. Then I carefully lifted *Red Wag 1* off the workbench and placed it inside the box, adding a few packing materials. Armed with my prized prototype, I was now ready to go.

Thanks to Grandpa, we got on the road at a decent time. The only problem was that heading straight east, the sun soon reminded me of what I had forgotten to bring with me on this trip – my sunglasses. And that was beginning to haunt me big-time. I fiddled with the sun visor, but it was barely adequate.

I was glad we were making this journey together, as there were a number of things I wanted to talk about. I decided to start by bringing up the conversation that had caught me off guard at Sunday's potluck.

"Grandpa, can we talk about your brother?" I glanced at Grandpa and saw his mouth settle into a thin line. Although I didn't want to upset him, I pressed on because I really wanted to know the story. "Either I had forgotten that you had an older brother who died in the war, or I never knew it. It doesn't seem like you've ever said much about him."

He sighed. "Well, Josh, it's not a nice story."

"Because it's about death? Give me a break; I can certainly handle that," I replied.

"No, not just that. The circumstances around it were a bit disturbing."

"I'd sure love to know, whatever they may be. If it is a family secret, you can trust me," I replied.

"Well, okay, I'll tell you the story. My brother, Don, was on a ship in the Pacific when it was attacked by Japanese warplanes. He was on duty, responsible for watching the radar screen. He was supposed to sound an alarm to warn everyone if he saw any blips on the screen. That way they could get quickly mobilized to respond."

"What happened?" I asked.

"We didn't find out the details until much later. Don was seriously injured and was taken to a hospital for a while. On top of all of his injuries, though, he was also really depressed. I'll never forget the day I visited him when he was in a state of delirium. All of a sudden he yelled out, 'Wake up, Don!' It took some work, but I was finally able to get the heartbreaking story out of him – he had fallen asleep on the watch, and didn't catch the blips of the incoming planes on the radar until it was almost too late. The ship survived the assault okay, but there was a lot of damage and a fair number of casualties, including a good buddy of Don's."

"So how long did your brother live?"

"Not too much longer, only a few weeks. I think it came down to him being so guilt-ridden that he didn't have much drive to continue living. No matter how much we tried to assure him that he had saved many lives, he could only think of the ones who didn't make it. War is just a sad, sad thing."

"That's really tough, Grandpa. I'm sorry. Were you and Don close?"

"It was hard. I did really look up to him a lot, and he had always taken me under his wing. I've never forgotten him, but as time passed it did become easier to manage the pain. We later found out that Don wasn't alone in this lapse. At Pearl Harbor, radar was actually installed on 19 warships before the Japanese attacked on December 7, 1941, but not one was turned on. Radar echoes were also detected from Hawaii 15 minutes before the attack, but were ignored, as authorities just assumed they were from some of our own planes. So it wasn't just Don who could have done a better job. I wish he had known this. It might have brought him some peace to know others had made mistakes as well. And as I said, it's such a shame he couldn't have thought more about how he used radar to save lives."

"I'm glad you told me that story," I said. It added a whole new dimension to my understanding of my grandfather.

We were passing by the exit to Worthington. Grandpa pointed off to the right.

"Over that way is where I used to teach – over at the vo-tech school," he said. "But I've given that up, too."

"I didn't know you were a teacher too," I exclaimed. Gosh, there was a lot more to my grandpa than I had ever known. "What did you teach?" I asked.

"I taught agricultural skills and mechanical arts at night – welding and that kind of stuff, y'know." That revelation only served to reinforce how little I really knew about my grandpa. I decided there was no better time to keep digging.

"You know," I continued, "there's something else I wanted to talk to you about. When I first got to Sioux Falls, you sounded somewhat irritated that it was just me, and not my parents, that had come down. Why?"

"Josh, please don't get me wrong," said Grandpa. "I couldn't be more thrilled that we've had this time together. But that doesn't mean I wouldn't also like to see the rest of my family. We've all grown so far apart."

He heard me begin to protest but continued, "Oh, I know your folks are concerned about me, but it would sure be nice if we had a closer relationship, like in the old days. What, here it's been about a year, and they haven't been down. In fact, the last several years, the visits have been pretty sparse. I get the feeling that if it weren't for my shaky health, they'd just continue on with their busy schedules. They can just send you down to check up on me."

"Yeah, I can see what you're saying. Sometimes I feel like I'm getting the short end of the stick, too. Dad is awfully busy with his career – climbing the corporate ladder. I guess that's his dream, but I do wish we were more connected like we used to be. It doesn't help that Marie is now part of the picture. It's always tougher when you have a stepmom who doesn't seem to be as interested in the old relationships."

With that, this seemed to be the perfect opportunity to bring up the other subject my dad had specifically asked me to address – would Grandpa consider moving to Minneapolis. I just couldn't put it off any longer, and since he was obviously seeking to improve the relationship, I thought this was probably a good time to broach the subject, although carefully.

"Grandpa, you know that episode on Friday really scared me. How often does that happen?"

"Oh, that's the first time in a long time – I just got too worked up all of a sudden."

"Aren't you worried it may happen again, and you won't be able to get help?"

"Nah, I've got my pills; I see a cardiologist regularly in Sioux Falls; I get plenty of exercise and watch my cholesterol levels; and there's always all my friends and neighbors nearby. The doctor says I'm doing everything I need to."

"So most of the time you feel good, with no chest pain?" I asked.

"Yeah, sure," he said without hesitation.

I tried to look him in the eye to see any hints of a less than candid revelation, but my angle was not good.

"You see, Dad and Mom are thinking it may be time for you to sell the farm and move to the Cities. What better way to help the relationship, as well?"

"Shoot. Yeah, I know; they've pushed that on me before, and even though it may help with the relationship, I'm not so sure it's about the distance. Besides, you think I'd be happy up there living in some apartment? I just don't want to do that."

"Well, we could find some nice place with a big garage that you could use as a workshop. You could still do your tinkering...I mean inventing."

"Nah."Grandpa shook his head firmly. "What it comes down to, Josh, is that if there is no real effort from them to connect, it wouldn't feel any different, especially with your stepmom now in the picture. Besides, think about it: I was born in my house, I've lived there my entire life, and I really don't want to leave it. My whole life is in southwest Minnesota – my friends and my church. I'm too old to start over."

"Okay, Grandpa, I can see you have strong ties down here. But if you keep working on your invention, and you keep striking out, you're going to have more episodes. Do you think you can keep dealing with all the failures of trying to be an inventor?"

"I have no problem plugging away. But since I haven't come up with anything yet, and my prospects don't look real good at this particular moment, it may take some work. My dream is still a work in progress. Like I've said, if you haven't invented anything, then you're just a tinkerer. I want to be an inventor, and there's no reason why I should stop trying."

"Grandpa, remember when you told me that one of the greatest joys inventors get is from improving the lives of other people? By that definition, you've done more than your share," I said earnestly. "Think of all the times you've come through for your friends and neighbors. Think of all the love and admiration you got Sunday morning at the tribute at church. You've been a key member of the community, and the last 69 years would not have been the same for them without you. Can't you take satisfaction in that?"

"Of course, but I can still have my dream to invent, right? What I really need to learn is not to wrap my whole life up into an invention, and not get so worked up if things don't go the way they're supposed to. I just have to keep remembering Mr. Bakken's remarks. Failure is just part of the journey, really just one step closer to success. I need to relax more on my journey."

"Yours has been a long one. Thanks to you, my journey has just begun, and I feel lucky to have an idea and a prototype that maybe just might work."

Grandpa smiled. "Yes, it's very exciting, Josh. But remember, there's a long way to go to turn it into what might be a viable product. I can help you to refine the design and build more prototypes, but you're going to have to get your dad engaged in the commercialization part. With his sales background, he should be able to check with the right people to see if there's a market for the *Red Wag*."

"I don't know," I said with a sigh. "Like I said before, getting

Dad involved might be a problem since he doesn't think I'm much of an inventive type."

"Well, just demonstrate it to him, and he can't help but get excited – especially with his interest in fish and aquariums. I'm sure he'll finally see that you've got some real ideas to offer. One bit of advice, though. Do it in your aquarium, not one of his. If you sucked up one of his fish by mistake, I don't think you'd be off to a very good start. It might bring back bad memories of other projects involving things like ketchup."

I knew Grandpa was gently poking fun at me, and I grinned. "Yeah, I wouldn't want to be the one to flush one of his precious fish down the toilet – especially one of those expensive saltwater beauties. Of course, I would hate doing that with any fish. Always makes me wonder – do they get to escape fish purgatory and end up in fish heaven?" Now Grandpa was laughing with me.

"Enough about fish!" I exclaimed. "Hey, where are we, anyway? How much further do we have to go?"

"You're sounding like some little kid," said Grandpa. "When are we going to get there?" Grandpa whined as if he were a 5-year-old. "Well, I could tell you exactly where we are at if I had one of those new GPS devices."

"Oh, yeah, I've heard of them. They sound so cool," I said. "I forget. What does GPS stand for?"

"Global Positioning System," said Grandpa. "They're still pretty pricey. I read where Garmin has a new model out called the

StreetPilot, designed just for travelers. But they cost about $700. That's too rich for my blood.

"Did you know," he continued, "that a Minnesotan was instrumental in developing the whole GPS system? Dr. Bradford Parkinson."

Grandpa went on to tell me about him. As an Air Force colonel, he was the one most responsible for sorting out the various navigational alternatives, and was ultimately able to validate the entire GPS concept back in the '70s. More than anyone, he convinced the government of its importance. It was at first strictly a military tool, requiring the government to make a significant investment in a multitude of satellites. But now that the infrastructure is in place, a lot of people are beginning to realize its commercial value.

"I'll tell you what," said Grandpa. "When the price of the commercial units comes down, I may just have to get one."

"Yeah, sounds like an awesome device." My mind drifted back to the purpose of our day trip. "But how about we talk some more about the guy we're going to see – Mr. Robert Page. You said you read his book and you've been doing a lot more research on him."

"You're right, there is a lot of fascinating information. Let's start with the basics. We kind of got into it when we were discussing bats. Do you know how radar works?"

"I think it's a matter of sending out a radio wave signal and measuring how long it takes to come back, right?" I queried.

"Basically, yes. The term 'radar' derives from the words Radio Detection and Ranging. It was actually a secret code word when it was first in development. In the mid '30s a number of countries were working on it in a race to make it a tool that could be used either militarily or commercially. That included the U.S., Britain, and Germany. In fact, some say the Germans were the first to use radio wave technology, but they made some strategic errors in not deploying it as a defensive tool. In the meantime, Sir Robert Watson-Watt, a Scotsman, was making great strides in development. Many people consider him the 'father of radar.' He originally proved out the concept, although the Americans were doing it at about the same time. But it was the man from St. Paul, Dr. Robert Morris Page, and two of his colleagues at the U.S. Naval Research Lab, Mr. Albert Taylor and Mr. Leo Young, who were able to improve it enough to make it a really functional tool during the war.

"For the first time, they were able to detect not only a target's existence, but also its range. Also, it used to be that the transmitter and receiver had to be placed some distance apart from each other, which made it almost impossible to use on ships, much less on airplanes. But Page's team developed the ability to use a smaller antenna plus a duplexer, combining the two into a single small unit. Now they could be installed on ships and in the noses of airplanes. The first successful sea trial of on-board radar was held in 1937. Then Page and his team also came up with a concept providing for continual updates in the form of pulses. Those pulses were captured as blips on the familiar round screens if something was sighted. Later, Page's team developed the first long-range radar for viewing over the horizon, more than 3,000 miles.

"By 1940, the Americans and Brits were collaborating on their efforts, creating Allied supremacy. Through clouds and total darkness, enemy ships were being sunk. A crowning day was in May of '43, when the Allied invasion sank more than 40 German submarines, also known as U-boats."

Sinking 40 submarines in one day? That seemed like quite a day's worth of work, I thought. You don't do that unless you've got some clear advantage. I thought back to the days when I used to play war with my GI Joe toys. Even on my best days, I don't think my guys were ever that good at overpowering the enemy.

Grandpa continued, "A more sophisticated development, called Microwave Early Warning (MEW), was made available for D-Day on June 6, 1944. The military installed it on the southern coast of England, and it provided a complete view of the entire battle. They could follow everything that was going on in the air and on the sea in real time."

"And to think, today when I hear about radar, it's mostly because of weather reports or navigation and things like that," I said. "I bet most people don't realize that it started out as such a valuable military tool."

"Yes, it was a remarkable invention with lots of benefits, "said Grandpa. "To think of everything that was accomplished when the pressure was on – not only by Page but also all those other Greatest Generation inventors we talked about." Grandpa shook his head slightly. "I look at how much you and I struggle to make our dreams a reality, and then I think of what they did – totally amazing. There is something else about Page, though, that makes me admire him even more than before."

"What's that?" I asked.

"Well, you often hear of scientists questioning their faith as they struggle to reconcile science and God. Page was just the opposite. Raised by a Methodist minister, he went out of his way after the war to write and lecture about his devout faith, showing a scientific basis for the relationships between science and scripture. He said that throughout his inventive career, there were many times when he would just get an inspiration. He would get a 'hunch' that a solution for something would work, and even without the slightest idea why, he'd be supremely confident that it would work. He believed that it was as if a source of knowledge out of this world had momentarily been opened to him, and he was guided by it."

"Amazing," I said. "But wouldn't some people just say that was intuition?"

"The concept of intuition has always puzzled me," Grandpa replied. "How can the human brain, based on past experience and knowledge, just get a feeling about answers to something unknown that's about to unfold in the future? To me it must be something much more. To me it is divine inspiration.

"Well, what I do know for sure," he went on, "is that his country rang the bell, asking him to serve in the best capacity he could, and he used all available means to not only try to answer it, but to do it exceptionally well, with great success. He was a true servant and patriot to his country. That's why I can't believe we are really getting this once-in-a-lifetime opportunity to meet him. I'm still pinching myself in disbelief!"

We were approaching an exit with some gas stations in view. "Let's get some gas and take a break," said Grandpa.

Once pulled in, I hopped out to fill up the tank. "Is there anything you want inside, Grandpa?"

"Yeah, get me a small Diet Coke with ice," he said, and handed me some money to cover it all.

Inside, I noticed a large pop and ice dispenser in the corner. Catching my eye was a familiar name on the label on the lower right corner of the machine with the name of an inventor he had told me about. "Hey Grandpa," I said while getting back into the truck. "I think I just ran into another Minnesota invention – the pop dispenser made by the Cornelius Company."

"Doesn't surprise me in the least," he said. "A person just doesn't realize how much all the Minnesota inventions impact our lives every day. And, as we have certainly talked about, throughout history."

We were soon back out on the freeway. Fortunately there had not been much traffic, so we were pretty much on schedule. As we were approaching Rochester, I began to reflect on all of the information I had learned about the great Minnesota inventors of our century. I wondered how a person goes about deciding who was the most important, so I asked my grandpa for his thoughts.

"Oh, that's a tough one," he said. "There are so many things you could look at – the most lives saved, the most number of people that use it, the greatest impact on making life and work easier, the most it advances science and technology, the longest time it has been used, the greatest bearing on history. I have no idea how you would go about deciding the order of importance. When you really get down to it, I think it's just an individual thing."

Chapter Ten

The Visit

"How far you go in life depends on your being tender with the young, compassionate with the aged, sympathetic with the striving, and tolerant of the weak and strong. Because someday in life you will have been all these."
—George Washington Carver, African American botanist and inventor

A s nursing homes go, this one seemed to be a rather nice one, not that I have much experience to speak of. I just remember visiting my great aunt Clara. This visit brought back memories of a distinct odor – the kind that seems to be part of the natural makeup of having a bunch of old people together in one place. Not that I had a big problem with that. After all, there were also some nice flower arrangements here and there, which helped to improve the atmosphere.

As we waited for the receptionist to get off of the phone, Grandpa couldn't help but comment, "It's so sad to think how many of our Greatest Generation have ended up stuck within four walls – pretty much ignored, except for maybe a few visits from family and friends. What is it about institutionalizing people that automatically means, 'The rest of the world, you can go on with your daily lives and pretty much forget about these folks?' Think of how many of these dear people die each day with only a handful of people knowing their stories."

Just then the gray-haired receptionist got off the phone and asked, "May I help you?"

"Yes, we're here to see Mr. Robert Page."

"Okay, please sign in, and I'll check," she said. She slid a clipboard and a pen across the counter toward us. She turned toward her desk and dialed the phone. When she hung up, she told us that the director would be with us in a moment.

"Mr. Page is such a nice man," the receptionist said. "It's just a shame that he can't talk."

Grandpa and I quickly glanced at each other. Uh-oh, we communicated silently.

"We heard he doesn't communicate well, but we didn't realize he doesn't speak. No words at all?" asked Grandpa.

"I think he's a stroke victim – he can vocalize a bit with a grunt or a chuckle, but I don't think he can form any words," she replied.

Grandpa took in a deep breath and pursed his lips. He then exhaled in a long, slow stream. The air had seemingly been snatched from his sails. Just then the director appeared, walking briskly around the corner and extending her hand to us as she introduced herself.

"Hello, I'm Sarah Anderson, the director here. You're not family of Mr. Page, are you?"

As we shook our heads, she continued, "I'm sorry to tell you that Mr. Page is no longer here – he was moved out yesterday evening after some medical complications developed. His niece was informed."

"Oh, no," said Grandpa. "What happened to him? Is it serious? Where is he now?" Concern creased his brow.

"I'm sorry," said Mrs. Anderson. "Medical privacy laws prevent me from sharing any of that information with you."

"What? You're telling me that after we've just driven three hours to see him there's no information you can give us? Can't you please help us out here?" Grandpa may have lost the wind in his sails, but that was not going to hold him back. The backup engine was now getting warmed up.

"I can see why you're frustrated," she said. "But, no, I'm sorry, I just can't tell you anything. It's policy."

"But Mrs. Anderson. You and I both know that policies have been bent in the past. Can't you make an exception? Why don't you just consider us family and be done with it. I need to know where he's at. Really, I do."

"I'm sorry, my hands are tied. I just can't help you," she said, and turned to walk away from us.

Grandpa's engine was now fired up. His face was turning red. "Come on, Josh, we're out of here," he muttered in disgust. He turned and strode to the entrance, banging the big door wide open to leave. I was close behind, not wanting to get hit on the backside by the return swing of that door.

"Relax, Grandpa," I said as we walked out. "Don't you think you need to take it easy?" I added somewhat timidly, not wanting to fuel the fires any higher.

"Yeah, I'm sorry. I kinda lost it there. Fine example I am for my grandson. As you know, patience is not one of my virtues."

"I understand – you're just so intent on finding Mr. Page." My spirits sank. I was starting to feel like maybe this would just turn into a wild goose chase. "So, now what do we do?" I asked.

"Well, they're not going to outsmart a Lindstrom. I have a hunch I know where he's at," said Grandpa. "If he has a medical condition, they probably sent him to the hospital. And if that's the case, it would be one of those hooked up with the Mayo Clinic, where he's been undergoing the therapy. I have a hunch he's at Rochester Methodist. Fortunately, I know it's just a short piece down the road here."

The ride to the hospital was a silent one, as Grandpa was clearly not in a talkative mood. He seemed to be on a mission, and nothing was going to interrupt him. I was okay with that. This was his big deal, and I was just along for the ride. About ten minutes later we pulled into the parking ramp at Rochester Methodist. We made a beeline to the information desk. Finding out his room number brought the first smile back to Grandpa's face. As for me, I had more of grin.

Coming off the elevator, we approached a middle-aged Hispanic woman at the nursing station to validate Mr. Page's whereabouts.

"Yes, that's right, he's in room 432, she said. "He's doing so much better today. We've stabilized him. We were just getting him sitting up and situated for lunch at 12:30. I think he'll be happy to have some visitors, but only for a short while. You do realize, though, that he can't talk? He's been a stroke victim for several years."

"Yes, we're aware of that. We won't take much of his time," Grandpa said.

As we entered his room, we caught sight of a thin, frail, bespectacled man with a pale visage. His head slowly lifted to acknowledge our presence, but he wore a puzzled expression – maybe he was disappointed we weren't bearing a tray with lunch.

"Hello, Mr. Page, I'm so glad to meet you," Grandpa said in a soft voice. "I'm Ralph Lindstrom, and this is my grandson, Josh."

Mr. Page lowered his chin in an almost imperceptible nod, and a slight smile lifted the corners of his mouth. It was a great relief to feel that we were at least viewed as welcome, and not intrusive. The bright sun shone through the window, adding to the upbeat feeling.

Grandpa moved to the side of the bed, but I stayed a bit behind, not wanting to overwhelm Mr. Page with two hulking presences (Okay, maybe I didn't qualify as "hulking," but I still thought it was polite not to crowd him.)

"Mr. Page, sir, I just wanted to come to meet you in person. I tracked down your niece, and she told us you were in Rochester. We've come all the way from southwest Minnesota – farm country," said Grandpa.

Mr. Page nodded his understanding, and with effort, gave us a verbal response, "uhhuh."

"Well, sir. There are just a few things I wanted to tell you in person – I promise not to take too much of your time. First of all, I deeply admire you and regard you as a great American hero. Everyone agrees that all your hard work on a radar solution during the war was critical to Allied success. Then, I'm totally amazed, that, with your backs against the wall, you were able to come through with critical developments like the duplexer based on just a hunch. I understand your team had that built and installed in a very short time. How long did it take?"

His hand shaking slightly, Mr. Page held up four fingers.

"Four weeks?" asked Grandpa.

Mr. Page slowly shook his head. He pointed to the sun outside the window and made a semicircle motion with his hand. I guessed he must have been indicating the sun's rising and setting.

"Oh, only four days?" exclaimed Grandpa. "That is totally amazing. Congratulations. So how long did it take to get it working once you tried it out?"

Mr. Page proudly held up just one forefinger.

"The very first time? asked Grandpa incredulously. "What an unbelievable story!"

That brought the biggest smile of appreciation and a louder "uhhhuh" from Mr. Page, along with a face filled with animation and color. For the first time, I noticed his eyes gleaming with life, as he recalled, I'm sure, some very memorable days. I couldn't help but think how sad it was that a man who knew a million times more than the sum of the square of the sides of an isosceles triangle was now relegated to communicating with just a few of his fingers.

"Second," my grandfather continued, "I want to commend you for sticking with a strong abiding faith that has guided your life. I know you've attributed a lot of your inventiveness to divine inspiration. And not only did you just believe, you also tried to tell others your story in the years following the war."

Mr. Page shook his head up and down with as much strength as he could muster.

"And finally, Mr. Page, I know several American presidents have honored you for your accomplishments. How many were there?"

Mr. Page nodded and held up four fingers – his face now

glowing like a harvest moon.

"So that must have been Truman, Eisenhower, Nixon, and, who was the fourth? Reagan, wasn't it? What an outstanding accomplishment – just wonderful." There was a slight pause as my grandpa tried to come up with his next sentence. He finally continued, "Well, there's no way I can match awards from presidents." His voice started to trail off, but then just as quickly rebounded. "But then there's one big thing I can do that is different. All that happened many, many years ago, right?" Grandpa waited for an acknowledgment from Mr. Page, which came as a nod.

"Well, I want to do something for you today, right here, right now, to show you you're not forgotten."

Grandpa pulled something out of his pocket and offered the object in his hand to Mr. Page. It looked like a medal of some sort. Aha, I thought, this must be what he was looking for in the attic last night.

"This, Mr. Page, is the Purple Heart medal awarded to my older brother, Donald, a Navy man who died in the war. He used your radar to save many lives on his ship before he was critically injured." Grandpa swallowed. "I think he would agree that this should now go to you."

Mr. Page's pale white fingers reached for the medal. With his trembling hand, he had some difficulty grasping it. Finally capturing the medal in his palm, he gazed at it for what seemed like a whole minute, and then clutched it tightly, bringing both steadiness and color back to his hand.

I could see the tears beginning to form at the corners of Mr. Page's eyes as they searched back up to find my Grandpa's eyes. But then, unexpectedly, he extended his arm out, as if to return the medal.

"Oh, no, no," said Grandpa. "I don't want it back. It's for you. Definitely, it's for you."

After a moment of silence, Mr. Page uttered, "Hmmm, hmmm," and then swiveled his head to look for me. He waved his other hand to beckon me forward, and I slowly approached his bedside.

He reached for my hand, turning it palm side up, and deposited the medal into it. With what must have been all of his strength, he squeezed my fingers tightly around it.

I quickly glanced back at Grandpa for some reassurance as to what to do. He was nodding his head as if to say, "That's okay; that must be his wish."

With that, Mr. Page turned my hand over and proceeded to do something I had never experienced from another man: He brought it slowly up to his lips, and kissed it. My glistening eyes caught his, no doubt revealing my gratitude, but at that very moment my mouth was frozen speechless. He then waved, appearing to signal it was time to say good-bye.

I will never forget Mr. Page's version of a good-bye: a kiss on the hand, a wave, a content smile, and a look of thanks – all wrapped up in one memorable point in time – so early in my lifetime, so late in his.

He beckoned my grandpa forward and, reaching out, gave him a kiss on his hand as well.

"We cannot thank you enough," said Grandpa, "for everything you have done. Good-bye, and God bless." Our eyes met his for a lingering moment, and we turned to leave the room.

*   *   *   *   *

For the first few minutes walking out, we were both in a quiet, reflective mood, trying to capture the full extent of what we had just experienced. As we left the hospital, I finally had to ask, "Grandpa, why did he want to give the medal to me? He doesn't know me, and I'm not even an inventor – at least not yet."

"That's not the point, Josh. I think he wanted to let you know that you're the next Great Generation. He just wanted to pass on his and Don's legacy to someone who will be continually reminded of what's important. If you can live your life like his, that's what counts. Also, it's a great remembrance of my brother, Don, whose service to his country should not be forgotten either. I'm glad that you have it."

I was having a hard time keeping my emotions under control. "I'm really honored to have it. I'll treasure it the rest of my life." But there was something else nagging me about our exchange with Mr. Page. After a moment of reflection, I just blurted it out: "You already knew the answers, right? All that business of you having him raise his fingers to those questions. You already knew that they built the duplexer in four days; it was successful on the very first try; and four presidents had honored him. You just asked him the way you did to pull him into the conversation, right?"

"I'm glad to see you're so perceptive," he replied. "You know, a guy in his position doesn't have too many opportunities to brag anymore. I figured if I could give him a chance to communicate in one of the few ways he's got left – what better way to let him show his well-deserved pride. I'll never forget, and will always cherish, the look on his face when he was able to hold up his fingers. They stood for some pretty incredible accomplishments."

"Very nicely done," I said. "You're always doing what's right for other people – from young to old. So did you plan to do it that way, or did it just come to you?" I asked.

"Oh, it just came to me in the moment. So maybe that makes it, what, – a mini-inspiration?"asked Grandpa.

"I suppose. I guess we all get mini-inspirations every once in awhile. But the medal part – that was totally planned, right?"

"Oh, yeah, you heard me up in the attic last night. I fully intended to give him Don's medal, but I wanted to keep it a surprise for you."

"You and your surprises," I grinned. That was pretty awesome on Grandpa's part to think of giving the medal to Mr. Page.

*   *   *   *   *

We were headed to the bus station in Grandpa's pickup. I

began thinking about how much I had benefited from this trip. I ended up as the recipient of all the knowledge and wisdom from Grandpa about Minnesota's great inventors. Then I had my very own idea turned into a prototype that I can show off to my dad. To top it off, I got to meet Mr. Robert Page and to keep this medal that had belonged to Grandpa's brother, a great uncle I never even knew I had.

I wasn't sure if I would be able to express my appreciation in the right way. "Thanks a lot for everything," I said. "I'm glad I came down – I got a real feel for what your life is all about, and how you're so respected in your community. That tribute at the church, the visiting afterward, and the food and all were amazing. On top of that, those dreams and contributions of Minnesota's great inventors that you told me about – they were unbelievable."

"As for Mr. Page, what can I say?" I added. "That was definitely a once-in-a-lifetime experience – meeting him, and getting sent off with a medal and a kiss on the hand – who could ask for more?" There was an extended silence as we both reflected on that wonderful experience.

Finally, Grandpa replied. "Well, what about building the prototype – you enjoyed doing that a little bit, didn't you?"

I broke out laughing. "Well, yeah; I was just messing with you, Grandpa. Of course, that was my favorite part. Turning my own idea into at least a half-working prototype – what unbelievable fun! Now I just have to get my dad on board to help me with the next step."

"You do that," he said. "Remember, I'll be here to help you in any way I can. I'll build the *Red Wag 2* with you. Gee, the three of us just might make a great team. You be the idea guy, I'll execute on the idea, and your dad can drive it home."

"What about your invention?" I asked. "You're going to continue to work on that, right?"

"You bet," he said. "That's my dream, and I'm going to keep at it. That's just the story of the life of an inventor."

Then something important flashed back into my mind. I was still thinking of the potential impact on his health. At the risk of pushing it a bit too far, I decided to ask. "Did you ever consider," I said with a pause, "that maybe it is just not meant to be? Maybe the invention won't ever work – and you'll be waiting forever to have the kind of inspiration Mr. Page had." No sooner had I said that than I was kicking myself, searching for a way to take it back.

There was more silence. I was hoping I hadn't hurt him, here, at the very end of our visit, with that candid question.

The silence lasted as we pulled into the bus station. Soon Grandpa was pulling up to the curb for departures. I didn't want to leave on a sour note, but I was struggling to come up with what to say next.

Finally, he spoke up. "Josh, who knows whether I'll ever come up with an invention – only God, I guess. If it comes down to an inspiration, I'm still trusting that it will come. But I intend to keep that dream alive, even if it means until the day I drop. As long as

I'm not hurting anybody else, I'll keep at it. If it makes you feel any better, though, tell your folks I promise to work more on my reaction to failure. I just have to keep relaxed if things don't go well, and hope for a better day. I have to remember Earl Bakken's words – that failure is closer to success than inaction. I think that's the sign of a real inventor."

"Okay, Grandpa, I get it. There's no denying a dreamer. But please give yourself more credit for your day-in and day-out interactions with other people – maybe a lot of them because of your mini-inspirations, as you called them. If that one big inspiration is just not meant to be, at least count up all the mini ones along the way. They're just as important, aren't they?" I couldn't think of any other way to express my thoughts. "Well, good-bye, Grandpa. I'll be thinking about you. Thanks again for everything."

"Sounds as if you've gained a bit of wisdom, Josh. Hey, I've really enjoyed having you around this weekend," he said. "Connecting with family is important. Hope all the inventor stuff wasn't too much, but I sure had fun building that prototype with you. You've got to agree that the meeting with Mr. Page was unforgettable, just as much for me as for you. At least I can say that one of my dreams was answered in a very special way for me today."After a moment of reflection, he added, "Maybe that means when you're here, good things happen. Come down more often, and next time, bring your parents."

"You know, Grandpa, I'm going to be sure to tell my folks that you could use a good dose of connected, expressed caring. I'm sure we'll all be checking up with you more often. And we have your big 70th birthday to look forward to! What can we get you? I don't imagine a set of Rollerblades would come in too handy on the farm."

"I don't know," he mused. "Do they come in an all-terrain version?" We grinned at each other.

"By the way," I continued, "I have one final request about your invention. Please let me be the first to know when it works. I'm sure that will be real soon."

"You've got yourself a deal," he said. "As long as you keep me up to date with what's going on with yours."

I grabbed my bag and the box with *Red Wag 1*, then gave him a hug. As I headed toward the large entry door to the bus station, I heard him yell out my name once again.

"Oh, and Josh, keep dreaming, kid."

Bibliography and Notes

Preface

1. Tom Brokaw, *The Greatest Generation* (New York: Random House, 1998).

2. "Minnesota Inventors Hall of Fame Inductees," accessed January 7, 2011, http://www.minnesotainventors.org/ inductees. For discussion throughout of all inventors except as otherwise noted.

3. Stephen George, *Enterprising Minnesotans – 150 Years* (Minneapolis: University of Minnesota Press, 2003), Foreword, x.

Chapter One

1. Diana, Princess of Wales. Great-Quotes.com, Gledhill Enterprises, 2010, accessed December 4, 2010, http:// www.great-quotes.com/quote/137066

2. "Lemelson-MIT Program," Inventor Archive, Charles Strite, accessed March 4, 2011, http://web.mit.edu/ invent/iow/strite.html

3. "The Antique and Classic Boat Society, Inc., Minnesota – Birthplace of Water Skiing" by Andreas Jordahl Rhude, accessed February 10, 2011, http://www.acbs-bslol.com/Porthole/BirthofWaterSki.htm

4. "Wikipedia for William Herbert Schaper," accessed February 10, 2011, http://en.wikipedia.org/wiki/Schaper_Toys

5. "NeatOldToys.com," Tonka Toy Trucks, accessed March 4, 2011, http://100megsfree3.com/lonestar/history.htm

6. The Reyn Guyer Agency of Design, accessed March 5, 2011, http://www.reynguyer.com/nerf.htm

7. About.com Inventors, "History of Rollerblades," Mary Bellis, accessed February 25, 2011, http://inventors.about.com/od/rstartinventions/a/Roller_Blades.htm

8. Kate Roberts, *Minnesota 150 – The People, Places, and Things that Shape Our State*

   (St. Paul, MN: Minnesota Historical Society Press, 2007). Discussion of Ron & Al Lindner and, in subsequent chapters, Adolf Ronning, Norman Borlaug, Walter Deubener, Owen Wangensteen, Seymour Cray, Frederick McKinley Jones, Robert Gilruth, and Bradford Parkinson.

Chapter Two

1. Dale Turner. Great-Quotes.com, Gledhill Enterprises,

2011, accessed May 11, 2011,
http://www.great-quotes.com/quote/38867

2. Martin Luther King gave his "I Have a Dream" speech on August 28, 1963.

Chapter Three

1. Henry Ford, BrainyQuote.com, Xplore Inc, 2011, accessed June 24, 2011, http://www.brainyquote.com/quotes/quotes/h/henryford121339.html

2. "Incredible People," Biography of Earl E. Bakken, accessed January 17, 2011, http://profiles.incredible-people.com/earl-e-bakken/

3. Lorraine Hopping Egan, *Inventors and Inventions* (New York: Scholastic, Inc., 1997), 13.

Chapter Four

1. Henry Bromel, *Northern Exposure,* "The Big Kiss," 1991, Quotation #32438 from Laura Moncur's Motivational Quotations, accessed April 12, 2011, http://www.quotationspage.com/quote/32438.html

2. Minnesota Inventors Congress and Resource Center, http://www.minnesotainventorscongress.org/

3. Feed My Starving Children, http://www.fmsc.org/page.aspx?pid=453

4. Chris Policinski, "Land O Lakes Makes Case for More Food" (Minneapolis *StarTribune,* March 6, 2011). Quoted as 250% increase in six decades.

5. Noel Vietmeyer, *Borlaug, Volume 3, Bread Winner, 1960 -1969* (Lorton, VA: Bracing Books, 2010), 48.

Chapter Five

1. Leonardo da Vinci. BrainyQuote.com, Xplore Inc, 2011, accessed June 2, 2011, http://www.brainyquote.com/quotes/authors/1/leonardo_da_vinci.html

Chapter Six

1. Thomas A. Edison. BrainyQuote.com, Xplore Inc, 2011, accessed May 6, 2011, http://www.brainyquote.com/quotes/quotes/t/thomasaed149049.html

2. Carol Pine and Susan Mundale, *Self-Made* (Minneapolis: Dorn Books, 1982), 50.

3. American Chemical Society, Division of Medicinal Chemistry, accessed May 6, 2011, http://www.acsmedchem.org/vince.html

Chapter Seven

1. Tom Brokaw, *The Greatest Generation* (New York: Random House, 1998), back cover.

2. Geoffrey C. Ward and Ken Burns, *The War: An Intimate*

History, 1941-1945 (New York: Knopf, 2007), 20, 84, 186, 300.

3. Robert Morris Page, *The Origin of Radar* (Garden City, NY: Anchor/Doubleday, 1962), 106-134.

4. John Megara, *Dropping Nuclear Bombs on Spain. The Palomares Accident of 1966 and The U.S. Airborne Alert* (Tallahassee: Florida State University, 2006), http://etd.lib.fsu.edu/theses/available/etd-04102006-115019/unrestricted/jmm_thesis.pdf

Chapter Eight

1. Earl Bakken, "Dreaming On," a publication of the Earl & Doris Bakken Foundation, accessed July 5, 2011, http://www.earlbakken.com/content/inspiration/dreaming.pdf

2. John S. Mailer, Jr., and Barbara Mason, Illinois Periodicals Online, "Penicillin: Medicine's Wartime Wonder Drug and Its Production at Peoria, Illinois," p. 42, accessed March 15, 2011, http://www.lib.niu.edu/2001/iht810139.html

3. BNET Business Publications, *Electronic News,* "Supercomputer Legend Seymour Cray dies at 71," by Sarah Cohen, Oct. 14, 1996, accessed March 24, 2011, http://findarticles.com/p/articles/mi_m0EKF/is_n2138_v42/ai_18783393/?tag=content;col1

4. Dr. Robert Morris Page actually died in Edina, MN, in May, 1992, of heart failure. See *New York Times* obituary by Bruce Weber, published May 18, 1992, http://www.nytimes.com/1992/05/18/us/robert-morris-page-is-dead-at-88-physicist-helped-to-refine-radar.html

5. Travis Brown, *Popular Patents* (Lanham, MD: The Scarecrow Press, 2000), 148-49.

Chapter Nine

1. Leo Tolstoy. Great-Quotes.com, Gledhill Enterprises, 2011, accessed Mach 4, 2011, http://www.great-quotes.com/quote/1885

2. Steven R. Strom, *An Interview with Dr. Brad Parkinson* (El Segundo, CA, 2003), http://www.aero.org/corporation/documents/ParkinsonInterview.pdf

3. The Spitfire Site, "Deflating British Radar Myths of WWII," contributor comments, accessed March 23, 2011, http://spitfiresite.com/2010/04/deflating-british-radar-myths-of-world-war-ii.html#comments

4. Memorial plaque as shown on Wikipedia, accessed March 24, 2011, http://en.wikipedia.org/wiki/File:Watson_watt_02_fr.jpg#globalusage

Chapter Ten

1. George Washington Carver. Great-Quotes.com, Gledhill Enterprises, 2011, accessed March 4, 2011.

http://www.great-quotes.com/quote/1370654

About the Author

D oug Cornelius, the son of one of Minnesota's most prolific inventors, Richard T. ("Dick") Cornelius, experienced early on the dreams of the consummate inventor. A graduate of Cornell University, Doug taught school, worked for the family business, and then spent 25 years procuring leading-edge technology for three Fortune 500 companies: 3M, American Express (Ameriprise), and Target. He lives with his wife in Brooklyn Park, Minnesota, and has two grown children and two grandchildren.

Dr. Robert Morris Page – radar

Earl Bakken with young inventor – pacemaker

Dr. Bradford Parkinson – GPS

R.T. Cornelius -- compressor; drink dispenser

Photo of Dr. Parkinson, as a military officer, in the public domain.

Arthur L. Fry – Post-it Note

Francis Okie – Wet/Dry Sandpaper

Photos courtesy of The Minnesota Mining and Manufacturing Company

Dr. Carl Miller – Thermo-Fax

Richard Drew – Scotch Tape

Photos courtesy of The Minnesota Mining and Manufacturing Company.

Patsy Sherman – Scotchgard

Dr. Norman Borlaug – hybrid wheat

Photo of Ms. Sherman courtesy of The Minnesota Mining and Manufacturing Company. Photo of Dr. Borlaug courtesy of the University of Minnesota Archives, University of Minnesota - Twin Cities.

Dr. Robert Vince – Herpes & HIV drugs

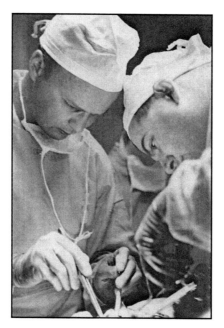

Dr. C. Walton Lillehei, Open Heart Surgery Process

Photographs courtesy of the University of Minnesota Archives,
University of Minnesota - Twin Cities.

Dr. Henry Buchwald, Implantable Infusion Pump

Dr. Owen H. Wangensteen, Gastric Suction System

Photographs courtesy of the University of Minnesota Archives,
University of Minnesota - Twin Cities

Appendix – "The Minnesota 80"

Alphabetical Listing of 80 of Minnesota's Greatest Inventors

1. Dr. Alexander P. Anderson

2. Earl E. Bakken

3. Dr. Norman E. Borlaug

4. Merton M. Bottenmiller

5. Dr. Henry Buchwald

6. LeRoy Buffington

7. Floyd E. Buschbom

8. Albert M. Butz

9. William L. Carlson, Jr.

10. Lynn L. Charlson

11. Franklin Chatfield

12. Richard T. Cornelius

13. Seymour Cray

14. Oliver Crosby

15. Herbert Francis Dalglish

16. Edward W. Davis

17. Richard V. DeLeo

18. Walter H. Deubener

19. Frank A. Donaldson

20. Richard G. Drew

21. Glen M. Dye

22. Carol M. Ford

23. Harold Fratzke

24. Harold Edward (Bud) Froehlich

25. Arthur L. Fry

26. Ebenhard S. (Gandy) Gandrud

27. Willis Gille

28. Robert Gilruth

29. John T. Gondek

30. Dr. Patrick R. Gruber

31. Reyn Guyer

32. Clifford L. Jewett

33. Bruce Johnson

34. Frederick McKinley Jones

35. Reuben A. Kaplan

36. Cyril Keller

37. Louis Keller

38. Mark W. Keymer

39. Joseph Killpatrick

40. Dr. Izaak M. Kolthoff

41. Carl G. Kronmiller

42. Dr. C. Walton Lillehei

43. Al Lindner

44. Ron Lindner

45. Henry G. Lykken, Sr.

46. Earl Masterson

47. William N. Mayer

48. Norman B. Mears

49. Dr. Carl Stinson Miller

50. Lowell A. Moe

51. Walter W. Moe

52. Dr. Alfred O. C. Nier

53. Carl W. Oja

54. Francis G. Okie

55. Brennan Olsen

56. Scott Olsen

57. Dr. Robert Morris Page

58. Dr. Bradford Parkinson

59. Melvin Pass

60. Ralph C. Peabody

61. B. Hubert Pinckaers

62. Daniel F. Przybylski

63. Adolf Ronning

64. Ralph Samuelson

65. William Herbert Schaper

66. Dr. Otto H. Schmitt

67. Patsy O. Sherman

68. Edwin Gustave Staude

69. Harold (Steve) Stavenau

70. Edward Streater

71. Charles Strite

72. D. Gilman Taylor

73. Joseph O. Thorsheim

74. Richard A. Thorud

75. Rose Totino

76. Takuzo (Tak) Tsuchiya

77. Dr. Robert Vince

78. Dr. Owen Harding Wangensteen

79. Harry Wenger

80. Dr. Frank D. Werner

Dr. Alexander P. Anderson – **Life:** (1862 - 1943)

Trade/Education: Botanist

Major Inventions: Process of using high pressure and superheated steam to cause corn starch in cereals to explode from guns – first used for puffed rice and wheat.

Patents: 25 U.S., 14 foreign

Major Affiliation(s): Quaker Oats Company

Other: Product first considered a confection like popcorn at the World's Fair in St. Louis in 1904. He also designed manufacturing equipment and conducted 15,000 related experiments.

Induction into Minnesota Inventors Hall of Fame: 1982

* * * * *

Earl E. Bakken – **Life:** (1924 -)

Trade/Education: Electrical engineer

Major Inventions: Transistorized, battery-operated, wearable external cardiac pacemaker; implantable pacemaker.

Patents: Unknown

Major Affiliation(s): Medtronic

Other: Pacemaker named one of 10 outstanding engineering achievements of last half of the 20th century by the NSPE. Bakken later received the Russ Prize, engineering's version of the Nobel, from the NAE. He also founded the Bakken Library and Museum.

Induction into Minnesota Inventors Hall of Fame: 1995

Dr. Norman E. Borlaug – Life: (1914 - 2009)

Trade/Education: Plant scientist

Major Inventions: Hybrid version of wheat that incorporated a shorter, stiffer body but held significantly more grain. It was especially resistant to disease and receptive to fertilizers.

Patents: Unknown

Major Affiliation(s): Rockefeller Foundation; University of Minnesota; Texas A&M

Other: Spent much time in Mexico, India, and Pakistan; increased wheat production, saving millions of lives globally. Winner of the Nobel Peace Prize in 1970, he was cited at his award ceremony for fighting famine "more than any other single person of this age."

Induction into Minnesota Inventors Hall of Fame: 2010

*   *   *   *   *

Merton M. Bottenmiller – Life: (1911 - 1997)

Trade/Education: Electrical engineer

Major Inventions: Spring and swivel mechanism for outdoor furniture; designed with body conforming wire construction, which made it very comfortable.

Patents: 12 **Major Affiliation(s):** Homecrest Industries, Inc.

Other: Additional patents on toys, dental equipment, and other furniture. Swivel outdoor furniture was distributed worldwide.

Induction into Minnesota Inventors Hall of Fame: 1991

Dr. Henry Buchwald – Life: (1932 -   )

Trade/Education: Prof. of Surgery and Biomedical Engineering

Major Inventions: Concept of intestinal bypass surgery to control cholesterol; infusion port and implantable pump for delivery of precise drug dosages.

Patents: Unknown

Major Affiliation(s): University of Minnesota

Other: Developed specialty devices including catheters, shunts, and sensors. Authored hundreds of articles and several books. Annual Buchwald Award established at the University of Minnesota to honor outstanding surgical residents.

Induction into Minnesota Inventors Hall of Fame: 1988

*   *   *   *   *

LeRoy Buffington – Life: (1847 - 1931)

Trade/Education: Architect; Engineer

Major Inventions: "Father of the Skyscraper" came up with the fundamental idea to erect steel frames and attach thin veneers, allowing for construction of much taller buildings.

Patents: 1 known **Major Affiliation(s):** Independent

Other: Patent claim for what he called a "Cloud-Scraper" at first disputed, but later confirmed by *American Architect* in 1929. Designed many significant buildings in Minnesota.

Induction into Minnesota Inventors Hall of Fame: 1996

Floyd E. Buschbom – Life: (1921 - 2002)

Trade/Education: Farmer-turned-inventor

Major Inventions: Bale loaders and silo unloaders.

Patents: 100+ U.S. & Canada

Major Affiliation(s): Van Dale, Inc.

Other: Invented other farm material-handling equipment including bunk and mixer feeders; feedlot accessories. Most of his inventions have become great labor savers, eliminating manual work.

Induction into Minnesota Inventors Hall of Fame: 1986

*   *   *   *   *

Albert M. Butz – Life: (1849 - 1904)

Trade/Education: Swiss immigrant

Major Inventions: "Damper flapper" (forerunner of the thermostat) was the first mechanism to control coal-fired furnaces.

Patents: 12

Major Affiliation(s): Butz Thermo-Electric Regulator Company (now Honeywell)

Other: It was the first application of the principle of feedback, upon which the science of automated controls was based.

Induction into Minnesota Inventors Hall of Fame: 1992

William L. Carlson, Jr. – Life: (1921 - 1989)

Trade/Education: Researcher; Engineer

Major Inventions: Pumps and valves

Patents: 31

Major Affiliation(s): University of Minnesota, DeZurick, Honeywell

Other: Stimulated the innovative thinking process in those working with him. Rare combination of educator, inventor, and mentor.

Induction into Minnesota Inventors Hall of Fame: 1981

* * * * *

Lynn L. Charlson – Life: (1909 - 2004)

Trade/Education: Self-taught engineer

Major Inventions: Low-cost hydraulic pump; hydraulic motor utilizing unique "generated rotor" principle called gerotor.

Patents: 94

Major Affiliation(s): Char-Lynn Company, later Eaton

Other: Great advances in fluid power arena, opening up uses in agriculture, mining, construction, and transportation where low cost, low speed, and high torque are required.

Induction into Minnesota Inventors Hall of Fame: 1985

Franklin Chatfield – Life: (1875 - 1973)

Trade/Education: Self-taught mechanical engineer

Major Inventions: Developed and improved knitting and fabric processing machinery.

Patents: 34 U.S. **Major Affiliation(s):** Munsingwear

Other: Researched shrinkage control and improvement of fabrics; established industry-wide standards. Joined with founder and inventor George Munsing to make Munsingwear a leader in the underwear industry in the 1900s.

Induction into Minnesota Inventors Hall of Fame: 1979

* * * * *

Richard T. Cornelius – Life: (1911 - 1978)

Trade/Education: Self-taught engineer

Major Inventions: Lightweight high-pressure air compressors; beer and soft drink beverage dispensing equipment, including concept of "premix" from a stainless steel tank.

Patents: 180 U.S., plus foreign

Major Affiliation(s): Cornelius Company in Anoka

Other: "Oil-less" diaphragm pumps; compressors used for skin-diving; Thermo-Serv insulated pitchers (with brother, Nelse); metal-inserted steak plates (with restaurateur Art Murray).

Induction into Minnesota Inventors Hall of Fame: 1980

Seymour Cray – Life: (1925 - 1996)

Trade/Education: Electrical Engineer; Computer Scientist

Major Inventions: Led design of first commercial supercomputer and subsequent faster models.

Patents: Unknown

Major Affiliation(s): Control Data, Cray Research, SRC

Other: When told that Apple had ordered a Cray, he said he ordered a Mac to develop the next Cray.

Induction into Minnesota Inventors Hall of Fame: Not inducted; however, inducted into the National Inventors Hall of Fame in 1997 and selected as one of the *Minnesota 150.*

*   *   *   *   *

Oliver Crosby – Life: (1855 - 1922)

Trade/Education: Engineer

Major Inventions: First large traveling cranes, hoisting devices, and wire rope clamps.

Patents: 36

Major Affiliation(s): Founded American Hoist and Derrick

Other: Applied crane designs to multiple industries, including railroad, lumber, sugarcane, and shipyards.

Induction into Minnesota Inventors Hall of Fame: 2005

Herbert Francis Dalglish – Life: (1911 - 1987)

Trade/Education: Self-made entrepreneur

Major Inventions: High-strength floating bridge support systems and pipeline couplings for military; heat-sensing bug detector for grain elevators.

Patents: 166 **Major Affiliation(s):** Dalglish Company

Other: Lawnmowers, material-handling equipment, and web-fed printing enhancements. Only two of his many patents failed to find a commercial market.

Induction into Minnesota Inventors Hall of Fame: 1983

*   *   *   *   *

Edward W. Davis – Life: (1888 - 1973)

Trade/Education: Professor

Major Inventions: "Mr. Taconite" developed the pelletizing process by which iron is extracted from taconite ore, which at one time was deemed worthless.

Patents: 19 U.S.

Major Affiliation(s): University of Minnesota

Other: Developed much of the mechanical equipment to commercialize the process, varying from furnaces to particle washers to conveyors; authored more than 50 publications to promote the industry, including internationally.

Induction into Minnesota Inventors Hall of Fame: 1979

Richard V. DeLeo – Life: (1922 -   )

Trade/Education: Aeronautical engineer

Major Inventions: Pioneer in air data measurement, including accurate altitude and velocity measurements for high-speed aircraft.

Patents: 16 **Major Affiliation(s):** Rosemount, Inc.

Other: Unique pressure pickup tube mounted outside the aircraft allowed for accurate measurements despite air turbulence close to the aircraft. Also, an author and valued mentor.

Induction into Minnesota Inventors Hall of Fame: 1986

*   *   *   *   *

Walter H. Deubener – Life: (1887 - 1980)

Trade/Education: Grocery store owner; Inventor

Major Inventions: First cord handles on shopping bags.

Patents: 1 known **Major Affiliation(s):** Unknown

Other: Received patent in 1919 and sold 1 million bags that year, 10 million in 1927. Other inventions include the "Jingleloon" musical balloon and a wastepaper compactor.

Induction into Minnesota Inventors Hall of Fame: Not inducted; however, selected as one of the *Minnesota 150.*

Frank A. Donaldson – Life: (1888 - 1945)

Trade/Education: Mechanical engineer

Major Inventions: Heavy-duty air cleaners, filters, and mufflers for tractors, combines, construction machinery, heavy-duty trucks, and military vehicles.

Patents: 22 **Major Affiliation(s):** Donaldson Company

Other: Product line expanded from intake to exhaust and grew to include over 4,000 items; company became the world's largest manufacturer of heavy-duty air cleaners, with over 10,000 employees worldwide.

Induction into Minnesota Inventors Hall of Fame: 1980

* * * * *

Richard G. Drew – Life: (1899 - 1980)

Trade/Education: Scientist

Major Inventions: Considered the "Father of the Scotch brand" of tapes, including masking and pressure-sensitive cellophane tapes.

Patents: Unknown **Major Affiliation(s):** 3M

Other: Tapes became 3M's second broad line of products. Designs evolved into many other types of tapes, including those made of a stronger, more flexible polyester.

Induction into Minnesota Inventors Hall of Fame: 1978. Also inducted into the National Inventors Hall of Fame in 2007.

Glen M. Dye – Life: (1884 - 1977)

Trade/Education: Postcard photographer

Major Inventions: Equipment to greatly automate the photo processing and X-ray industry.

Patents: 45 U.S. **Major Affiliation(s):** Pako Corporation

Other: Developed a color film-processing machine specifically for Disney Studios for creating cartoons, and an auto X-ray processing machine for the Mayo Clinic to provide progress reports during operations.

Induction into Minnesota Inventors Hall of Fame: 1984

*   *   *   *   *

Carol M. Ford – Life: (1956 -   )

Trade/Education: Physicist; Engineer

Major Inventions: Major enhancements to the ring laser gyroscope, extending its life with upgraded cathodes and allowing for sizes as small as a quarter.

Patents: 12 U.S. **Major Affiliation(s):** Honeywell

Other: Long life of RLGs allowed for their use on Space Station Freedom. Later developed a gyroscope with an expected life of over 114 years.

Induction into Minnesota Inventors Hall of Fame: 1994

Harold Fratzke – Life: (1929 -   )

Trade/Education: Farmer; Inventor

Major Inventions: Spring-loaded covers for tractor hydraulic ports, preventing contamination.

Patents: About 50 **Major Affiliation(s):** Full-time farmer

Other: Developed Hydra Levers to open ports, Roto-Chopper for shredding stalks, and low-cost release devices for hydraulic couplers – most manufactured by companies in southwest Minnesota. High commercial success rate – over 50%.

Induction into Minnesota Inventors Hall of Fame: 1994

*   *   *   *   *

Harold Edward (Bud) Froehlich – Life: (1922 - 2007)

Trade/Education: Engineer

Major Inventions: Deep submergence research vessel named ALVIN; stratospheric balloons and environmental sampling equipment; surgical equipment including skin staplers; mechanical arms for the nuclear industry.

Patents: 17 **Major Affiliation(s):** General Mills, 3M

Other: ALVIN was capable of dives to 14,760 feet below sea level. It's still operational after 4,664 dives over 47 years, including retrieval of a bomb and the remains of the *Titanic*.

Induction into Minnesota Inventors Hall of Fame: 2011

Arthur L. Fry – Life: (1931 -   )

Trade/Education: Scientist

Major Inventions: Post-it notes

Patents: 71 **Major Affiliation(s):** 3M

Other: Design evolved into many other repositionable products. Adhesive that was once considered a failure is now used in more than 300 other applications, such as bandages and decorating kits.

Induction into Minnesota Inventors Hall of Fame: 2002. Also inducted into the National Inventors Hall of Fame in 2010.

*   *   *   *   *

Ebenhard S. (Gandy) Gandrud – Life: (1902 - 1988)

Trade/Education: Pipestone County Agent

Major Inventions: Rod-measuring wheel; applicators for accurate spreading of fertilizers, chemicals, herbicides, and insecticides.

Patents: 80 **Major Affiliation(s):** The Gandy Company

Other: Honored by the U.S. government for his many contributions to American agriculture.

Induction into Minnesota Inventors Hall of Fame: 1984

Willis Gille – Life: (1905 - 1970)

Trade/Education: Electrical engineer

Major Inventions: Control mechanisms utilizing electronic temperature control principles; developed the first three-axis electronic autopilot installed on 30,000 bombers.

Patents: More than 85 **Major Affiliation(s):** Honeywell

Other: Developed a silent solenoid and a gun stabilizing system used on Army tanks. His inventions were the impetus for Honeywell to grow into a diversified industrial giant.

Induction into Minnesota Inventors Hall of Fame: 1976 (first inductee)

*   *   *   *   *

Robert Gilruth – Life: (1913 - 2000)

Trade/Education: Aeronautical engineer

Major Inventions: Designed the Mercury capsule and its propulsion systems, plus directed subsequent NASA projects.

Patents: Unknown **Major Affiliation(s):** NASA

Other:. Led Gemini program; responsible for spacecraft design and astronaut selection and training. He directed a total of 25 crewed space flights.

Induction into Minnesota Inventors Hall of Fame: Not inducted; however, selected as one of the *Minnesota 150*.

John T. Gondek – Life: (1911 - 2006)

Trade/Education: Self-taught hydraulic engineer

Major Inventions: Hydraulic gear and hoists for loading ammunition on Navy ships; numerous types of postwar hydraulic gear and related manufacturing tools.

Patents: Unknown

Major Affiliation(s): Northern Ordinance; Gondek; Oildyne

Other: Long-running hydraulic controls; medical inoculation guns; auto-opening davenport beds; pumps for fast-food-dispenser cleaning; electric outboard motor.

Induction into Minnesota Inventors Hall of Fame: 1997

*   *   *   *   *

Dr. Patrick R. Gruber – Life: (1960 -   )

Trade/Education: Chemist

Major Inventions: Commercially viable process for producing polyactic acid (PLA), a biodegradable plastic made from starches from cornstalks or wheat.

Patents: 48 U.S. **Major Affiliation(s):** Cargill Dow LLC

Other: Resultant plastic performs as well as petroleum-based resins, reducing dependence on foreign oil. It is recyclable and biodegradable and also uses 30-50% less energy to produce, creating fewer harmful greenhouse gases.

Induction into Minnesota Inventors Hall of Fame: 2003

Reyn Guyer – Life: (1935 -   )

Trade/Education: Designer; artist; sculptor

Major Inventions: Nerf balls

Patents: Unknown

Major Affiliation(s): Reynolds Guyer Designers

Other: Nerf balls inspired from foam packing materials. Other contributions included Twister game, Wrensong Music, Winsor Learning Inc., *Curly Lasagne* stories and songs.

Induction into Minnesota Inventors Hall of Fame: Not inducted.

*   *   *   *   *

Clifford L. Jewett – Life: (1909 - 1986)

Trade/Education: Research chemist

Major Inventions: Two distinct areas of contribution: methods to artificially color granules used in asphalt shingles, and the first pre-sensitized metal lithographic printing plates.

Patents: 7 U.S. **Major Affiliation(s):** 3M

Other: Ceramic-coated roofing granules provided longer life and multiple color choices; low-cost printing plates helped speed industry change from letterpress to offset printing.

Induction into Minnesota Inventors Hall of Fame: 1987

Bruce Johnson – Life: (Dates unknown)

Trade/Education: Mechanical designer for electronics

Major Inventions: Breathe Right nasal strips

Patents: 1 known

Major Affiliation(s): Creative Innovation & Design; CNS

Other: Had tried various internal means of opening the nostrils; finally, an architectural building design inspired his idea to pull externally with semi-rigid strips.

Induction into Minnesota Inventors Hall of Fame: Not inducted.

*   *   *   *   *

Frederick McKinley Jones – Life: (1893 - 1961)

Trade/Education: Self-taught mechanic, engineer

Major Inventions: Developed the refrigeration systems used on trucks, trains, and ships.

Patents: More than 60 U.S.

Major Affiliation(s): Thermo King Company

Other: Invented a portable X-ray machine; automatic ticket taker; sound-track movie projector, auto-starting gas engine.

Induction into Minnesota Inventors Hall of Fame: 1977; also inducted into the National Hall of Fame in 2007, member of the *Minnesota 150*, honored by President George H. W. Bush.

Reuben A. Kaplan – Life: (Dates unknown)

Trade/Education: Entrepreneurial inventor

Major Inventions: Universal gear puller; wide selection of mechanics' tools; high-pressure fluid power puller.

Patents: 15 U.S.

Major Affiliation(s): Owatonna Tool Co., later OTC

Other: Major supplier of tools to the military during WWII; received multiple awards. Also developed ultra-high-pressure fluid power technology.

Induction into Minnesota Inventors Hall of Fame: 1989

*   *   *   *   *

Cyril and Louis Keller – Life: (Born: 1922;1923 -)

Trade/Education: Agricultural blacksmiths

Major Inventions: Bobcat, the first true four-wheel-drive skid-steer loader, with wheels with the least load allowed to "skid," making it very agile.

Patents: Unknown

Major Affiliation(s): Melroe, later Ingeroll-Rand

Other: Bobcat made *Fortune* magazine's list of top 100 "America's Best" products.

Induction into Minnesota Inventors Hall of Fame: 2004

Mark W. Keymer – Life: (1908 - 2001)

Trade/Education: Engineer

Major Inventions: Specialty sheet metal hand tools.

Patents: Unknown

Major Affiliation(s): Malco Products, Inc.

Other: Tools had unique features such as compound leverage capability and cushioned, nonslip grips that were color-coded for easy identification. Company now is employee-owned.

Induction into Minnesota Inventors Hall of Fame: 2007

*   *   *   *   *

Joseph Killpatrick – Life: (1933 -   )

Trade/Education: Engineer

Major Inventions: The ring laser gyroscope – a sensor made out of light beams instead of rotating wheels – used for navigation that helps guide, steer, and stabilize airplanes.

Patents: 40 U.S., plus foreign

Major Affiliation(s): Honeywell Military Avionics

Other: Many innovative manufacturing, cost-saving, and life-extension ideas for the ring laser gyroscope.

Induction into Minnesota Inventors Hall of Fame: 1995

Dr. Izaak M. Kolthoff – Life: (1894 - 1993)

Trade/Education: Professor Emeritus of Analytical Chemistry, University of Minnesota

Major Inventions: Synthetic rubber development

Patents: Unknown

Major Affiliation(s): University of Minnesota

Other: Chief force in developing analytical chemistry as a modern science. Published thousands of papers, many about concepts of analytical methods of iodometry and potentionmetry, as well as concept of pH (alkalinity vs. acidity).

Induction into Minnesota Inventors Hall of Fame: 1985

*   *   *   *   *

Carl G. Kronmiller – Life: (1889 - 1968)

Trade/Education: Electrical engineer

Major Inventions: Modern-day thermostat ("Mr. Thermostat"); safety device for fuel burners using pilot light.

Patents: 71 **Major Affiliation(s):** Honeywell

Other: The actual round design of the thermostat was credited to a colleague, Henry Dreyfuss, and its shape was trademarked. Kronmiller also invented a multi-wall cement bag.

Induction into Minnesota Inventors Hall of Fame: 1988

Dr. C. Walton Lillehei – Life: (1918 - 1999)

Trade/Education: Cardiac surgeon

Major Inventions: Pioneered processes related to open heart surgery, including "cross circulation" with donors, the pacemaker with Earl Bakken, and the heart-lung machine.

Patents: Several

Major Affiliation(s): University of Minnesota

Other: Contributed to invention of certain artificial heart valves; authored over 600 technical papers; trained more than 150 cardiac surgeons.

Induction into Minnesota Inventors Hall of Fame: 1993

* * * * *

Al and Ron Lindner – Life: (Dates unknown)

Trade/Education: Fishermen

Major Inventions: Lindy Rig fishing bait concept for walleyes

Patents: Unknown

Major Affiliation(s): Lindy Tackle Company

Other: Developed *In-Fisherman* magazine, television and radio shows; Lindy sinkers; and other related fishing aids. Promoted concept of catch-and-release philosophy.

Induction into Minnesota Inventors Hall of Fame: Not inducted; however, selected as one of the *Minnesota 150.*

Henry G. Lykken, Sr. – Life: (1880 - 1958)

Trade/Education: Agricultural engineer

Major Inventions: Fine-grinding and separating equipment for a diverse group of industries: flour; candy, cosmetics, pigment, and coal pulverizing.

Patents: Unknown (dozens)

Major Affiliation(s): Strong-Scott Company

Other: Fine-grinding process for flour allowed it to retain more protein. Also invented a pneumatic grain elevator; emergency tire; tiles and furnace design.

Induction into Minnesota Inventors Hall of Fame: 1978

*   *   *   *   *

Earl Masterson – Life: (1916 - 2002)

Trade/Education: Self-taught electromechanical engineer

Major Inventions: Enhancements to video cameras and cassette recorders; major peripherals for early large mainframe computers, such as printers, tape drives, and mass storage.

Patents: More than 60 U.S.

Major Affiliation(s): Univac; Honeywell

Other: Invented automated microscope for analyzing white blood cells; sound-creating device to aid cystic fibrosis patients.

Induction into Minnesota Inventors Hall of Fame: 1997

William N. Mayer – Life: (1930 -   )

Trade/Education: Electrical engineer

Major Inventions: Magnetic thin film technology; plasma displays for computers.

Patents: 28 U.S.

Major Affiliation(s): General Mills; CDC; Modern Controls (Mocon)

Other: Developed pharmaceutical weighing instruments, plastic membrane thickness measurement instruments, and oxygen detection systems. *Forbes* named his company, Mocon, one of 200 Best Small Companies (1988 – 91)

Induction into Minnesota Inventors Hall of Fame: 1998

*   *   *   *   *

Norman B. Mears – Life: (1904 - 1974)

Trade/Education: Entrepreneur

Major Inventions: Photomechanical reproduction capabilities creating etched sighting devices during wartime and later mass production of aperture masks for color televisions.

Patents: 25 U.S., plus foreign

Major Affiliation(s): Buckbee-Mears Company

Other: Instrumental in developing Lowertown St. Paul; cited by Chamber of Commerce, with park named after him.

Induction into Minnesota Inventors Hall of Fame: 1993

Dr. Carl Stinson Miller

Life: (1913 - 1986) **Trade/Education:** Physical chemist

Major Inventions: Thermo-Fax duplicating machine utilizing special paper – first sold in 1949 to the CIA.

Patents: 18 **Major Affiliation(s):** 3M

Other: First "machine" marketed by 3M. Concept drove growth of overhead transparency projector business; replaced by xerography in the 1970s.

Induction into Minnesota Inventors Hall of Fame: 2009

*   *   *   *   *

Lowell A. Moe

Life: (1916 - 2003) **Trade/Education:** Electronics engineer

Major Inventions: Electronic measuring and control apparatus for food and grain handling, including unique ultrasonic device for repelling rodents in food and grain storage areas.

Patents: 70 U.S. and foreign

Major Affiliation(s): American Engineering; Peavey

Other: Key developer of enhancements to microwave radar and sonic blind landing altimeters during WWII.

Induction into Minnesota Inventors Hall of Fame: 1990

Walter W. Moe – Life: (1913 - 1997)

Trade/Education: Farmer; Inventor

Major Inventions: Power-driven post hole digger; cornstalk cutter and sheller.

Patents: Unknown

Major Affiliation(s): Montevideo Mfg. and Metal Company

Other: Invented a power egg washer, a bolt and drill measuring device, and a hydraulic tandem truck axle. Awarded two consecutive grand prizes at the Minnesota Inventors Congress.

Induction into Minnesota Inventors Hall of Fame: 1990

*   *   *   *   *

Dr. Alfred O. C. Nier – Life: (1911 - 1994)

Trade/Education: Regents' Professor of Physics

Major Inventions: Pioneered use of mass spectrometer to weigh atoms, recommending to the Manhattan Project that uranium-235 be used rather than U-238 for the first atom bomb.

Patents: Many

Major Affiliation(s): University of Minnesota

Other: Used mass spectrometers to measure geological age. Involved with NASA team and Viking mission to Mars, devising equipment and experiments.

Induction into Minnesota Inventors Hall of Fame: 1982

Carl W. Oja – Life: (1917 - 1992)

Trade/Education: Businessman; Manufacturer

Major Inventions: Four-footed walking cane; stretchers and tables such as SpineGuard and the Rescue Board.

Patents: 14 **Major Affiliation(s):** ACTIVEAID, Inc.

Other: Expanded line to include chairs for invalids and numerous products for hospital rehab and home health care. Actively engaged in helping other inventors.

Induction into Minnesota Inventors Hall of Fame: 1987

*   *   *   *   *

Francis G. Okie – Life: (1880 - 1975)

Trade/Education: Manufacturer of printing inks and powders

Major Inventions: "WetorDry" sandpaper

Patents: Unknown **Major Affiliation(s):** 3M

Other: Product was developed by his own company, then submitted to 3M, who soon hired him. Waterproof sandpaper eliminated safety and health hazards as well as clogging.

Induction into Minnesota Inventors Hall of Fame: 1980

Brennan and Scott Olsen – Life: (Dates unknown)

Trade/Education: Hockey-playing brothers

Major Inventions: Enhanced design of inline skates with polyurethane boots and wheels, as well as first heel brakes.

Patents: Unknown

Major Affiliation(s): Rollerblade Company

Other: Rollerblade Company has developed many improvements, including a lighter resin, Active Brake Technology, and buckles.

Induction into Minnesota Inventors Hall of Fame: Not inducted.

*　*　*　*　*

Dr. Robert Morris Page

Life: (1903 - 1992) **Trade/Education:** Physicist

Major Inventions: Pulse radar system; duplexer combination transmitter and receiver; Plan Position Indicator (PPI), showing both direction and range of target as blips on round screen.

Patents: More than 75

Major Affiliation(s): U.S. Naval Research Laboratory

Other: Radar I.F.F. (Identification – Friend or Foe); first long-range, over-the-horizon radar (3,000 miles); fire control radar; Microwave Early Warning (MEW).

Induction into Minnesota Inventors Hall of Fame: 1979

Dr. Bradford Parkinson – Life: (1935 -   )

Trade/Education: Engineer; Educator

Major Inventions: Considered "father" of the Global Positioning System, which uses 24 satellites to aid users in determining their precise location.

Patents: 7 known

Major Affiliation(s): U.S. Air Force, Stanford Univ.

Other: Promoted further uses of GPS such as for blind aircraft landing systems and robotic tractors. Awarded the Draper Prize, considered engineering's equivalent to the Nobel Prize.

Induction into Minnesota Inventors Hall of Fame: Not inducted, however inducted into the National Inventors Hall of Fame in 2004 and selected as one of the *Minnesota 150*.

*　　*　　*　　*　　*

Melvin Pass – Life: (1908 - 2004)

Trade/Education: Manufacturing engineer

Major Inventions: Improved safe manufacture of munitions and their recovery and disposal.

Patents: Unknown

Major Affiliation(s): U.S. Ordinance Corp.; Twin Cities Arsenal

Other: During WWII, improved processes for safe manufacture of munitions, later developed machinery to salvage them. Also developed systems for "mothballing" machinery for use during later wars, as well as a portable mechanical degreaser.

Induction into Minnesota Inventors Hall of Fame: 1996

Ralph C. Peabody

Life: (1920 - 2000) **Trade/Education:** Engineer

Major Inventions Vacuumized power sweeper

Patents: 9 **Major Affiliation(s):** Tennant Company

Other: By mechanizing a menial task, contributed to safer, more productive workplaces, leading to improved employee morale. Other products include scrubbers, carpet extractors, buffers, and polishers.

Induction into Minnesota Inventors Hall of Fame: 1981

*   *   *   *   *

B. Hubert Pinckaers – Life: (1924 -   )

Trade/Education: Electrical engineer

Major Inventions: Temperature controls; solid state electronic controls and instrumentation.

Patents: 80 U.S. **Major Affiliation(s):** Honeywell

Other: Pioneered development of solid state components (electrons flowing through unheated solid semiconductors), which are far more reliable than vacuum tubes.

Induction into Minnesota Inventors Hall of Fame: 1987

Daniel F. Przybylski – Life: (1917 - 1978)

Trade/Education: 8th grade plus Dunwoody Institute

Major Inventions: Trenching and ditch digging equipment; HOPTO digger, backhoe, and crane.

Patents: 44 U.S., plus foreign

Major Affiliation(s): Archer Daniels Midland; Badger Machine Co., later Warner & Swasey Co.

Other: Also invented the Sky Draulic Zoom Boom.

Induction into Minnesota Inventors Hall of Fame: 1999

*   *   *   *   *

Adolf Ronning – Life: (1893 - 1982)

Trade/Education: Farmer-turned-inventor

Major Inventions: Ensilage harvester (with brother Andrean); "Farmall System of Horseless Farming."

Patents: Dozens

Major Affiliation(s): Business sold to International Harvester

Other: Inventions included headlight dimmers; golf course mowers; stick control for tanks.

Induction into Minnesota Inventors Hall of Fame: Not inducted; however, selected as one of the *Minnesota 150.*

Ralph Samuelson – Life: (1904 - 1977)

Trade/Education: Agriculture

Major Inventions: Water skis (first demonstrated on Lake Pepin in 1922)

Patents: None

Major Affiliation(s): Self employed – involved in ski demos and farming

Other: Never filed for a patent; that he was first was later attributed to him in 1966. Also performed ski jumping and ski flying.

Induction into Minnesota Inventors Hall of Fame: Not inducted.

*　　*　　*　　*　　*

William Herbert Schaper – Life: (1914 - 1980)

Trade/Education: Postman-turned-inventor, manufacturer

Major Inventions: Cootie game

Patents: Unknown

Major Affiliation(s): Schaper Mfg., later Milton Bradley

Other: Original design whittled from a fishing lure. Sold 1.2 million Cootie games from 1949 to 1952. Invented other games such as Ants in the Pants, Tickle Bee, and Dunce.

Induction into Minnesota Inventors Hall of Fame: Not inducted.

Dr. Otto H. Schmitt – Life: (1913 - 1998)

Trade/Education: Professor Emeritus – Physics, Bio, and Electrical engineering – three Ph.D.s

Major Inventions: Trigger that allows a constant electronic signal to be changed to on/off state.

Patents: Unknown

Major Affiliation(s): University of Minnesota

Other: Fundamental electronics such as emitter followers and differential amplifiers; many war contributions, including the Manhattan Project jointly with his wife.

Induction into Minnesota Inventors Hall of Fame: 1978

*   *   *   *   *

Patsy O. Sherman – Life: (1930 - 2008)

Trade/Education: Research chemist

Major Inventions: Led the development of the first stain repellent and soil release textile treatments known as Scotchgard.

Patents: 16 U.S., plus foreign **Major Affiliation(s):** 3M

Other: Original intent was to develop a new rubber for jet fuel hoses, when accidental discovery was made. Applied concept to permanent press, wool, upholstery, and carpeting.

Induction into Minnesota Inventors Hall of Fame: 1989. Also inducted into the National Inventors Hall of Fame in 2001.

Edwin Gustave Staude – Life: (1876 - 1964)

Trade/Education: Farmer; Inventor

Major Inventions: Paper box making machinery; envelope making machinery

Patents: 143 U.S. and foreign

Major Affiliation(s): E.G. Staude Mfg. Co.

Other: Later manufactured tractors and related equipment including power brakes and fluid drive transmissions. Other inventions included phonographs and garage door openers.

Induction into Minnesota Inventors Hall of Fame: 1991

* * * * *

Harold "Steve" Stavenau – Life: (1920 -   )

Trade/Education: Engineer

Major Inventions: Window hardware, including the lever lock operator that revolutionized awning window mechanisms.

Patents: 10 U.S.

Major Affiliation(s): Truth Tool Co. (Truth, Inc.)

Other: Focused on production efficiencies to make Truth the world's largest producer of window hardware, including a full line of lever locks, hinges, and operators.

Induction into Minnesota Inventors Hall of Fame: 2000

Edward Streater – Life: (Dates unknown)

Trade/Education: Lumber Retailing

Major Inventions: First steel steam shovel and crane and clam that became forerunners of Tonka toys.

Patents: Unknown

Major Affiliation(s): Streater Industries sold design to Mound Metalcraft, later Tonka Toys, now part of Hasbro.

Other: Decided to sell toy inventions because did not like prospect of trying to market them.

Induction into Minnesota Inventors Hall of Fame: Not inducted.

*   *   *   *   *

Charles Strite – Life: (1897 - 1960)

Trade/Education: Mechanic

Major Inventions: Time-activated and spring-loaded mechanism for popping up toast.

Patents: 1 known

Major Affiliation(s): Waters Genter Co.; Edison (Toastmaster)

Other: Design grew from frustration of getting burnt toast at the company cafeteria.

Induction into Minnesota Inventors Hall of Fame: Not inducted.

D. Gilman Taylor – Life: (1902 - 1981)

Trade/Education: Engineer

Major Inventions: Temperature and instrumentation controls for airplanes and other industrial applications.

Patents: 62 U.S., plus foreign

Major Affiliation(s): Honeywell

Other: Invented high-acceleration motors; gyroscopic controls; low-cost angular rate measuring devices for aircraft autopilots; and centrifuge for blood separation.

Induction into Minnesota Inventors Hall of Fame: 1980

*   *   *   *   *

Joseph O. Thorsheim – Life: (1906 - 1986)

Trade/Education: Physicist; Engineer

Major Inventions: First effective hydrogen-oxygen fuel cell controls used commercially in industry and then in space; auto exhaust analyzer used by Ford to minimize air pollution.

Patents: More than 18 U.S.

Major Affiliation(s): Honeywell

Other: Wide variety of other designs: reflective body bands for bicyclists, measurement devices to optimize plant growing cycles, and aids for respiratory illnesses.

Induction into Minnesota Inventors Hall of Fame: 1990

Richard A. Thorud – Life: (1922 -   )

Trade/Education: Engineer

Major Inventions: Enhancements to many lawn and snow care products, emphasizing safety, efficiency, and environmental friendliness, including improved grass mulching.

Patents: 35 U.S., 17 foreign

Major Affiliation(s): Toro Corporation

Other: Pioneered industry-wide safety standards for lawn mowers. His invention of the "Power Curve Rotor" for single-stage snow throwers dramatically increased their performance.

Induction into Minnesota Inventors Hall of Fame: 2011

*   *   *   *   *

Rose Totino – Life: (1915 - 1994)

Trade/Education: Pizza entrepreneur

Major Inventions: Developed a pizza crust suitable for freezing that retained its crispness. The secret was frying, rather than baking, before freezing.

Patents: 1 known

Major Affiliation(s): From Totino's pizza shop to Totino's Finer Foods, later Pillsbury/General Mills

Other: Major philanthropist who gave millions to local schools, church, and charities.

Induction into Minnesota Inventors Hall of Fame: 2008

Takuzo (Tak) Tsuchiya – Life: (1918 - 1999)

Trade/Education: Mechanical engineer

Major Inventions: Continuous puffing gun that improved capacity, quality, and consistency of ready-to-eat cereals.

Patents: 21

Major Affiliation(s): General Mills

Other: Invented low-vibration conveyors, fish cutters, process for clam-shucking, and texturizing vegetable protein for meat substitutes.

Induction into Minnesota Inventors Hall of Fame: 1992

*   *   *   *   *

Dr. Robert Vince – Life: (Dates unknown)

Trade/Education: Professor of Medicinal Chemistry

Major Inventions: Two monumental antiviral medications: Acyclovir treatment for herpes and a "carbovir"-based compound marketed as Ziagen by GlaxoSmithKline to treat HIV.

Patents: 23

Major Affiliation(s): University of Minnesota

Other: Royalties coming back to the University are estimated to exceed $400 million as of 2010. These funds are used for additional research, an endowment for grad students, and a new drug center.

Induction into Minnesota Inventors Hall of Fame: 2010

Dr. Owen Harding Wangensteen – Life: (1898 - 1981)

Trade/Education: Professor Emeritus of Surgery

Major Inventions: Gastric suction system used to aspirate gas and fluid from stomach and intestines via a tube through the nose.

Patents: Unknown

Major Affiliation(s): University of Minnesota

Other: Developed freezing technique for ulcers; surgical instruments. Esteemed teacher and trainer of many open heart surgeons, including Christian Barnard and C. Walton Lillehei.

Induction into Minnesota Inventors Hall of Fame: 1983

*   *   *   *   *

Harry Wenger – Life: (Dates unknown)

Trade/Education: Music teacher; Inventor

Major Inventions: Equipment to improve music education, including choral risers, music stands, acoustical shells, cabinets, and stages.

Patents: Unknown

Major Affiliation(s): Wenger Corporation

Other: Invented a snare drum practice pad and sousaphone chair. Company is now the world's leading manufacturer of equipment for music education and performing arts.

Induction into Minnesota Inventors Hall of Fame: 2001

Dr. Frank D. Werner – Life: (1922 -   )

Trade/Education: Engineer

Major Inventions: Air data sensors for measuring outside temperatures and pressure on almost all commercial and military jet airplanes. Also, significant applicability to NASA space requirements such as Apollo missions, including moon landing.

Patents: 77 U.S., plus foreign.

Major Affiliation(s): Co-founded Rosemount

Other: Invented ski boots, windshield repair process, and unique golf club design.

Induction into Minnesota Inventors Hall of Fame: 2006

CPSIA information can be obtained at www.ICGtesting.com
Printed in the USA
BVOW072346160212

283081BV00001B/4/P